Bazil & Lydia Osgood
Sunday, March 23, 1930

Bazil & Lydia Osgood
Sunday, March 23, 1930

BY

TRACY WILSON

http://beautifulpublications.com

Published by
Beautiful Publications LLC
Stratford, CT 06614

PRINT ISBN: 978-1-7343353-1-6
EBOOK ISBN: 978-1-7343353-2-3

Printed in the United States of America

Dear Mom & Dad,

Dad, you loved Mom with all your heart. You were very loving and compassionate. Mom, you loved Dad with all your heart too. As a child, I would watch you both be affectionate, and loving, and I would often tell myself when I got married, I was going to be just like Dad and I was going to have a wife just like Mom.

When you died, I took it hard – not only because I was sad you both weren't with me any longer, but also because I still hadn't found my wife. I was sad because I wasn't able to show you that I had a love like yours. I grieved for the loss of both of you, I grieved for the loss of my wife, and I grieved for your daughter-in-law you never got to meet.

If anybody had told me not to worry because I would see you again and you would meet your daughter-in-law, I would've been afraid that as soon as I got married, I'd be dead. Never in a million years would I have imagined that you would come back from the dead, ask for my help, we'd be able to help you, and you'd meet your daughter-in-law.

Thank you for coming back.

Love always, your Son, Bazil

"Mi Lydia ... te necesito por favor ... Mi Lidia... I need you... please..."

"Bazil ... yo también te necesito ... Bazil... I need you too..." she breathed as she clung to me...

"Mi Lydia ... te sientes tan bien ... todavía te sientes bien ... incluso en la muerte ... Mi Lydia... you feel so good... you still feel good... even in death..." I breathed as I laid her down in the grass...

"Sí Bazil ... hazme el amor ... te anhelo ... Yes Bazil... make love to me... I crave you..."

"No entiendo... I don't understand..." I breathed as I kissed her... "Estoy muerto ... pero todavía muy vivo ... I'm dead... but still very much alive..." I breathed as I took my dick out my pants...

"Sí Bazil ... te quiero ... soy tuyo en la vida ... y en la muerte ... hazme el amor ... por favor ... Yes Bazil... I want you... I'm yours in life... and in death... make love to me... please..."

1

"Si mi Lydia ... Yes Mi Lydia..." I breathed as I eased myself inside her...

"Oh Bazil ... Sí ... Eso es ... No te detengas ... Oh Bazil... Yes... That's it... Don't stop..."

"Mi Lydia ... tu coño se siente como la noche en que hicimos el amor por primera vez ... Mi Lydia... your pussy feels just like the night we made love for the first time..." I said as I started thrusting...

"Bazil ... ¿cómo es esto posible? Bazil... how is this possible?"

"No me importa... I don't care..." I breathed as I kissed her hard and fucked her deeper...

"Huh... Huh... Huh... Huh..."

"Uuugh! Uuugh! Uuugh! Uuugh!"

"Bazil ... me estoy acabando... Bazil... I'm cumming..."

"Cum para mi ... Cum for me..."

"Haah... Haah... Haah... Haah... HAAAAAH!"

"Uuugh! Uuugh! Uuugh! Uuugh! UUUUUGGGGHHHH!"

"Te quiero mucho... I love you so much..." Lydia said as she started crying...

"Mi Lydia..." I breathed as I kissed her eyes... "Por favor ... no llores ... Please... don't cry..."

"No puedo evitarlo ... me temo ... I can't help it... I'm afraid..."

"Yo te protegere... I'll protect you..."

"Nuestro nieto está en la ventana ... Our grandson is in the window..."

"Lo sé... I know..."

"¿Por qué no le dirá a su padre? Why won't he tell his father?"

"Es un niño ... tiene miedo ... He's a child... he's afraid..."

"¿Qué pasa si Bazil nunca viene? What if Bazil never comes?"

"Bazil vendrá ... lo prometo ... Bazil will come... I promise..."

"Quiero confiar en ti... I want to trust you..."

"¿Te he decepcionado alguna vez? Have I ever let you down?"

"No pero... No... but..."

"Mi Lydia..." I breathed and then I kissed her again... "Te amo ... por favor ... confía en mí ... I love you... please... trust me..."

"Te amo ... por favor ... confía en mí ... I love you... I want to be with you always..."

"Vas a... You will..."

"Deseo que la Corporación de Paisajismo nunca haya creado ese fertilizante ... I wish the Landscaping Corporation never created that fertilizer..."

"¿No me siento bien contigo? Don't I feel good to you?"

"Sí Bazil ... te sientes bien conmigo ... pero me siento Clayton ... y él no se siente bien ... y estoy asustada ... Yes Bazil... you feel good to me... but I feel Clayton... and he doesn't feel good... and I'm scared..." she said as she started crying again...

"No Mi Lydia... Por favor... please..." I breathed as I kissed her... "Sienteme... Feel me..." I breathed as I eased myself inside her again...

"Bazil ... Sí ... te siento ... Bazil... Yes... I feel you..." she moaned as I covered her mouth with mine, put my tongue in her mouth, tongued her down, and fucked her harder and deeper...

"Mmmm! Mmmm! Mmmm! Mmmm!"

"Mmmph! Mmmph! Mmmph! Mmmph!"

"Mmmm! Mmmm! Mmmm! Mmmm! MMMMMMMM!"

"Mmmph! Mmmph! Mmmph! Mmmph! MMMMMMMPPPHHHH!"

"Bazil ... para ... Bazil... stop..."

"Mi Lydia ... por favor ... te sientes tan bien ... no me hagas parar ... Mi Lydia... please... you feel so good... don't make me stop..." I breathed as I pulled out of her, lifted her dress, and began kissing her down her body...

"Bazil ... oh si ... Bazil... oh yes..." she moaned. I continued kissing my way down, spread her legs, and dove in...

"BAAAZZZIIILLLL!" she moaned as she grabbed my head with her hands and locked her legs around my head... "Aaah... Aaah... Aaah..." she was coming in my mouth, her nectar was sweet, and I was thirsty... "AAAAAAGGGHHHH!" I continued licking, sucking, and slurping until she spoke...

4

"Bazil ... él viene ... Bazil... he's coming..."

"No, Mi Lydia ... te protegeré ... No Mi Lydia... I'll protect you..."

"Bazil ... nuestro hijo está aquí ... Bazil... our son is here..."

"Oh, mierda! Oh shit!" I exclaimed as I jumped up off Lydia, helped her up, we fixed our clothes, and waited for our son to come into the backyard...

"Hello Bazil..." I said...

"What the fuck — am I high?!" Bazil exclaimed...

"What the hell took you so long?" Lydia asked...

"Mom? Dad?"

"Yes Son..." I answered...

"What are you doing here?" Bazil asked...

"We need your help..." Lydia answered...

"Mom... Dad... how..."

"Bazil — we don't have a lot of time..." Lydia said...

"Mom... please..." Bazil said as he started crying...

"Bazil..."

"Yes Dad?"

"We need your help..."

"You're DEAD!" Bazil snapped... "I'm ALIVE! My son is scared to death! Why are you here?"

"BAZIL!" I boomed...

"Yes Dad..."

5

"We didn't mean to scare Jay..."

"How the fuck do you know his name?"

"Bazil... he's our grandchild..." Lydia said...

"Your grandchild thinks you're monsters!"

"Bazil – we tried to get your attention – but he saw us... and you didn't..." Lydia said...

"You wanted to get my attention by fucking in my backyard?"

"Bazil – we're running out of time – you're running out of time..." I said...

"Running out of time – wait a minute – am I dying?"

"No son – you're not dying... not yet..."

"What the fuck is that supposed to mean?"

"They're coming..." Lydia answered...

"Who's coming?"

"Zombies..."

"Troy – stop playin!" Bazil laughed...

"Troy's not here..." I said...

"Stop... I can't..." Bazil laughed...

"GOT DAMMIT BAZIL WILL YOU LISTEN!" I boomed...

"Sure... I'll play along... I'll listen... tell me all about the zombies..." he laughed...

"The Landscaping Corporation developed a new fertilizer..." Lydia explained...

"What does fertilizer have to do with zombies?" Bazil laughed...

"When people use this new fertilizer... it gets absorbed into the ground – once you water it – you trigger something in the fertilizer that wakes us up... and..." I explained...

6

"And what?"

"We wind up in backyards... or graveyards... or parks... fucking through eternity..." I sighed...

"Wait a minute — you're telling me that this fertilizer wakes up the dead — and makes you fuck?"

"It doesn't make us fuck — but we're dead — we can't control our urges..."

"My son drew a picture for his teacher..." Bazil started to explain..."

"I know... I'm sorry..."

"You're sorry? What the fuck am I supposed to do? What if they school sends an investigator to our house because they suspect we're abusing him?"

"Bazil — you need to tell them to stop using the fertilizer... before it's too late..."

"Sure Dad — I'll just call the Landscaping Corporation — I'll tell them I had a conversation with my dead parents — who told me about the fertilizer — and when they ask me if I was hallucinating I'll tell them I have proof — because my son caught them fucking in my backyard!"

"Bazil... please... help us... help all of us..." Lydia pleaded...

"I CAN'T!" Bazil yelled...

"Son... please... you have to do this..."

"And you have to get the fuck outta my backyard!" Bazil yelled as he swung the bat and I caught it and snatched it from him...

"BAZIL — LISTEN!" I boomed...

"Yes Dad?"

"They'll be others... once they see the others... they'll believe you..."

"Others?"

"We have to go now... we love you... kiss our grandchildren..." Lydia said as we went back into the hole in the grass and disappeared.

"I'm Scott McGee, Anchor and Managing Editor, News 12 Westchester. We interrupt our regularly scheduled programming to bring you this report. We go live to Tara Rosenblum..."

"Thank you Scott. I'm here with a woman who wishes to remain anonymous... go ahead Maam..."

"They're fuckin' in my backyard!" she exclaimed...

"Excuse me – Maam?"

"The zombies – they're in my backyard – I called the police – they wouldn't come!"

"Maam – where are the zombies?"

"I'll show you..."

"Ladies and gentlemen – the following video should not be viewed by children..." Scott said as the video was played...

"Maam – when was this video taken?" Tara asked...

"It was taken last night! I called the police – they said I'm crazy so my husband took this video!"

"Well Scott – there you have it – Erotic Zombies – back to you..."

"We'll continue to update you on this bizarre story as it develops. In the meantime – residents are being warned to lock your doors before dark and stay indoors after sunset. We now return to our regularly scheduled programming..."

"I'm gonna calls News 12..." Chandler said as he picked up his phone...

"You've reached Gwen Edwards, News 12 Connecticut – how may I help you?"

"This is Sergeant Chandler Corbett of the Bridgeport Police..."

"Do you have a story for me Sergeant Corbett?"

"I need to see you right away – if you agree to see me – you'll get an exclusive..."

"Can you meet me at 28 Cross Street in Norwalk?"

"Give me 30 minutes..." Chandler said and then he hung up... "Let's go!" he said as they left the precinct...

"Nice to see you Sergeant Corbett – Mr. Osgood – how are you?" Gwen asked as she extended her hand to shake his...

"Nice meeting you – can we go inside?"

"All of you?"

"All of us..." Bazil answered...

"This must be big..." she said as she led them all inside...

"Bazil Osgood – I thought that was you!" Della Crews beamed when she saw him...

"Hello Della..."

"You two know each other?" Gwen asked...

"Bazil and I go way back... isn't that right Bazil?" Della answered...

"We've gotta go – they're here to give me an exclusive..." Gwen said...

"An exclusive! Okay then! Right this way!" Della beamed as she escorted us all to Gwen's office. Once they were inside, Bazil got up to close the door...

"What's going on?" Della asked...

"The sooner we give Gwen the exclusive, the sooner you'll find out..." Bazil answered before closing the door...

"Wow... ummm..." Gwen started to say...

"Are there any recording devices in here?" Bazil asked...

"I'd like to record this – unless you'd prefer to be off the record..."

"I don't mind being on the record – I just want to make sure the only one that has to hear what we say is us..." Bazil said...

"I'd like this to be on camera... if that's alright..."

"That's fine with me – is it fine with you guys?" Bazil asked...

"I didn't know we was gonna be on camera..." Keisha said...

"Is that a problem for you?" Gwen asked...

"I guess it's aiight..." she said...

"Okay – let's get started..." Gwen said as she set up the camera. Once it was set to record, she hurried back over to her seat...

"We're recording in five, four, three, two, one... Good evening – I'm Gwen Edwards, Reporter, News 12 Connecticut. Tonight I'm here with Bazil Osgood, President and CEO of Osgood Publishing to bring you an exclusive – Go ahead Mr. Osgood...

"Earlier this week, my son was woken out of his sleep by noise in my backyard...

"Was there a break in?"

"I looked out the window... and I saw... zombies..."

"Mr. Osgood – is this some type of publicity stunt?"

"Ms. Edwards – I wouldn't be sitting here with Sergeant Corbett of Bridgeport, Sergeant Hurley of Milford, my wife, or my neighbors if I were trying to get publicity – unless I was being arrested..."

"I'm sorry – you said you saw zombies..."

"Yes – I saw them out the window..."

"How did they get in your backyard?"

"They came up through the grass..."

"What where they doing there?"

"Once I went out into the backyard... I realized the zombies were my parents..."

"Your parents?"

"My parents were there to ask for my help... and to warn me..."

"What do your parents need your help with?"

"My parents need you to contact the Landscaping Corporation and tell them they need to stop producing their new fertilizer..."

"Why would your parents... wait a minute – are you saying this new fertilizer wakes up the dead?"

"Once you water your plants, there's an ingredient in the fertilizer and once that gets absorbed into the soil... it wakes up the dead... and..."

"What Mr. Osgood?"

"The zombies aren't able to control their sexual urges..." Bazil sighed...

"Oh my God..." Gwen said...

"We've started getting reports from residents in Milford claiming that they've seen zombies having sex in their backyard..." Sergeant Hurley said...

"I also took a couple of reports today in Bridgeport claiming the same thing..." Chandler said...

"We didn't actually see any zombies – but my husband could tell something went down in our backyard..." Keisha said...

"What's your name Maam?"

"I'm Keisha Cochran – this is my husband, Troy..."

"Mr. Cochran – what did you see when you went in your backyard?"

"It looked like something came up out the dirt..."

"Have you been in your backyard since?"

"No..."

"Mr. Osgood – you said your parents were there to ask for your help – and to warn you..."

"Yes..."

"What was the warning?"

"Zombies are coming..."

"I have a backyard – I like to entertain – do I need to be afraid?"

"They only come out at night – but after what I saw in Troy's backyard... you won't want to entertain..."

"This is Gwen Edwards, Reporter, News 12 Connecticut and you're watching an exclusive interview where we've just learned Erotic Zombies have been observed by residents here in Fairfield County..." she said before she turned off the camera... "Mr. and Mrs. Osgood, Sergeant Corbett, Sergeant Hurley, Mr. and Mrs. Cochran – I want to thank you for this exclusive..."

"You're welcome..." Chandler said...

"See yourselves out – I gotta run!" she yelled as she ran down the hall...

"This is Della Crews, Anchor, News 12 Connecticut. We interrupt our regularly scheduled programming to bring you this exclusive. We now turn to Gwen Edwards..."

"Mr. Osgood!" the reporters came running along with their cameras as soon as they saw them, giving Keisha and Troy an opportunity to run inside...

"When was the first time you saw your parents?"

"How long have your parents been zombies?"

"Have you always seen ghosts?"

"Are you psychic?"

"How many times have your parents visited?"

"Have you contacted the Landscaping Corporation?"

"Have you seen zombies during the day?"

"How do you know they can't control their sexual urges?"

"Mrs. Osgood – have you seen the zombies? We're you scared?" Bazil took Beautiee by the hand and started to pull her away from the

15

cameras but when she started speaking he changed his mind...

"Yes, I've seen his parents in our backyard..." she answered as the cameras flashed...

"Were you scared?"

"I'm not afraid of his parents..." she answered...

"Were they having sex when you saw them?"

"Yes they were..."

"Uh uh! Get these cameras away from these kids!" Chandler snapped...

"This is Della Crews, News 12 Connecticut. Earlier this evening, the Osgoods were spotted going into the Holiday Inn, where we were able to get a few comments from Mrs. Osgood..."

"Mrs. Osgood – have you seen the zombies? We're you scared?"

"Yes, I've seen his parents in our backyard..."

"Were you scared?"

"I'm not afraid of his parents..."

"Were they having sex when you saw them?"

"Yes they were..."

"Uh uh! Get these cameras away from these kids!" Chandler snapped...

"What's that? Hang on...we've just been notified that Erotic Zombies have been spotted at McLevy Green, downtown Bridgeport. Gwen

Edwards is live on the scene – Gwen – what can you tell us?"

"Della – it's crazy – as you can see behind me – officers are attempting to block the area by taping it off as some of the officers are fighting off the zombies..."

"Did you say fighting? The officers are actually fighting?"

"The officers are attempting to block the zombies from leaving and the zombies are attempting to push back – oh shit..."

"Gwen? Gwen are you there? We've lost contact – we'll be back momentarily – we'll keep you posted..."

"Sarge..."

"What the hell? Thompson?"

"Yea..."

"What the hell – never mind – I'm not talkin' to you – you're dead!"

"I'm sorry..."

"Get the fuck outta here!" Chandler snapped...

"You think I wanna be here?"

"Why the hell are you here?"

"Sarge – hurry – before it's too late!" Jermoll said and then he went back in the dirt along with the other zombies.

"Is it bad?" Beautiee asked, already knowing the answer...

"It's bad..." Bazil sighed as he pulled her into a hug and they held each other...

"I made you a promise earlier..." she whispered...

"Yes... you did..."

"I'd like to keep that promise..."

"I'd like that too..."

"Come with me..." she said as she took him by the hand and led him into the living room... "Sit..." she commanded. Bazil sat down on the couch and smiled at her mischievously. She stood there looking at him for a few moments before she moved closer to him and stood in front of him. Bazil reach up and grabbed her by her hips and then she spoke... "Don't..." Bazil put his hands down and smiled as she grabbed the pillows on the end of the couch, dropped them on the floor, kneeled on them, and spread his legs...

"Yeesss..." he breathed as she unbuckled his belt and unzipped his pants. Instead of taking his dick out with her hands and stroking it, she put her head between his legs and tortured him by moving his dick around with her tongue before taking it in her mouth...

"Bazil! ¿Qué estás haciendo? Bazil! What are you doing?" Lydia whispered...

"Shhh..." I whispered as she came closer and we peeked through the window...

"Dios mío, ¿deberíamos dejar que terminen? Oh my God — should we let them finish?"

18

"Ojalá pudiéramos ... pero nos estamos quedando sin tiempo ... I wish we could.... but we're running out of time..."

"Me recuerda a nosotras ... Reminds me of us..." Lydia laughed...

"Lo sé, sería muy tranquilo ... comenzarías a chuparme la polla ... ¡y BAM! ¡Aquí había venido tocando a la puerta! I know – it would be so quiet... you'd start suckin' my dick... and BAM! – here he'd come knocking on the door!" I laughed...

"Hmmm, eso me da una idea ... Hmmm – that gives me an idea..." she said as she knelt down and took my dick out my pants...

"Mi Lydia ... tus manos ... se sienten tan bien ... Mi Lydia... your hands... they feel so good..."

"¿Cómo se siente esto? How does this feel?" she asked as she took my dick in her mouth...

"Mi Lydia... Oooohhh...." I moaned as I grabbed her head with my hands and fucked her mouth. I was moaning so loud I probably woke up the entire neighborhood – but I didn't care – this was the first time I'd felt my wife's mouth since we died – and in that moment I wasn't in my son's backyard – I was in heaven... "Mi Lydia - ¡Soy CUUMMIINNGG! Mi Lydia – I'M CUUMMIINNGG!" I boomed as my body convulsed...

"Me sabes tan bien ... You taste so good to me..." she breathed as she continued sucking for a

19

few moments and then I started crying... "Me sabes tan bien ... Bazil... my love... no..." she whispered as she stood up, wrapped her arms around me, and held me... "Te amo ... por favor no llores ... I love you... please don't cry..."

"Mi Lyida ... me haces sentir tan bien ... Quiero quedarme aquí para poder sentirte por siempre ... Mi Lydia... you make me feel so good... I want to stay here so I can feel you forever..."

"Bazil ... mi amor ... me sentirás por siempre ... Bazil... my love... you will feel me forever..." she breathed as she pulled me into a kiss...

"Mi Lydia ... te amo ... Mi Lydia... I love you..."

"Bazil ... yo también te amo ... Bazil... I love you too..."

"Tenemos que decirles ahora ... We have to tell them now..."

"Si... Yes..." she said as we moved over to the French doors and started knocking...

"Beautiee..." he moaned as he grabbed her head and pushed his dick in further...

"Mmm... hhmmm..." she moaned on his dick as he fucked her mouth..."

"Tick... tick... tick..."

"Bazil..."

"Yes... Beautiee..." he moaned...

"What's that noise?"

"Tick... tick... tick..."

"Let me go check..." Bazil said as he jumped up and went to the kitchen. When he didn't come back right away, Beautiee came to get him...

"Mom... Dad..." Bazil said as he opened the French doors..."

"Bazil... I'm sorry..." I said as Bazil stepped out into the backyard. Beautiee walked into the kitchen and stood by the door so she could continue to hear our conversation...

"What's wrong?" Bazil asked...

"We ran out of time..." Lydia said as she started crying...

"Mi Lydia ... por favor no llores ..."

"Mi Lydia... please don't cry..." his father said as he wiped her tears...

"I did what you said..." Bazil said as he started crying...

"Yes... you did... but it's too late..." I said...

"Tell me what to do... let me try and fix it..." Bazil cried... "Please..." At this point, Beautiee started crying too...

"Clayton always wanted me..." Lydia said...

"I don't understand..." Bazil said...

"He tried to force me to be with him... but your father took care of that..."

"You killed him?" Bazil asked...

"Yes..." I answered...

"Once he was dead... we were free to live our lives... we were happy... we had you... and we could be together in eternity... as long as he was dead... but now..." Lydia said and then she started crying again...

"Mom..."

"Mi Lydia..." I whispered as I took her face in my hands and kissed her...

"He's awake..." Bazil sighed...

"It's not just that..." Lydia said as she continued crying...

"Clayton is angry..." I said...

"He's coming for you... isn't he?" Bazil asked...

"He's coming for both of us..." Lydia cried...

"What can I do?" Bazil asked...

"Clayton is the Alpha..." I answered...

"What does that even mean?"

"It means he's controlling all the other zombies – including your parents..." Beautiee answered as she stepped outside into the backyard...

"Beautiee..." Bazil whispered...

"Beautiee – I'm so sorry..." Lydia cried...

"Beautiee – don't!" Bazil yelled as he tried to stop her from hugging his mother...

"You're not afraid of me?" Lydia asked...

"No..." Beautiee answered as they hugged each other...

"Dad..." Bazil cried as he ran to hug me...

"Hello Bazil..." I said as Bazil cried in my arms... "Stop crying and go hug your mother..." I laughed. Bazil went over to hug his mother and Beautiee came over to hug me...

"I've wanted to do this ever since I saw you... but I was afraid..." Bazil cried...

"We'd never hurt you..." Lydia said...

"We'll do whatever it takes..." Beautiee said...

"I know you will – I've seen what you're capable of..." I laughed... "I wish we got to know you before we died..."

"So do I..." Beautiee said...

"As happy as I am to be having this reunion, we need to talk..." I said...

"What's wrong?" Bazil asked...

"Clayton is close..."

"Oh damn..."

"The other zombies are a distraction..." Lydia said...

"He wants to eliminate me... so he can have your mother in eternity..." I said...

"How can he eliminate you?" Bazil asked...

"By crushing my skull..."

"I won't let that happen..." Bazil gritted...

"He's too strong... you can't fight him..." Lydia said...

"Yes... we can..." Beautiee said...

"Beautiee – you don't understand..."

"Mom – we got this..." she said...

"See Lydia – I knew I was right about her..." I said...

"Beautiee – I love you – but I'm scared for you..." Lydia said...

"We'll be alright..." she said...

"My grandchildren need you..." Lydia said...

"And I'll be there for them..."

"Damn I love you..." Bazil said as he pulled her into a kiss and kissed her hard...

"I'm Scott McGee, Anchor and managing Editor, News 12 Westchester. We've just received word that Erotic Zombies have been spotted in Oakland Cemetery. We now go to Tara Rosenblum at Oakland Cemetery – Tara – what can you tell us?"

"Scott – I can't go anywhere near the entrance – can you see what's going on behind me?"

"Tara... is that what I think it is?"

"Yes Scott – the zombies are wreaking havoc, running around... and having sex..."

"Wait a minute – I'm getting something..." Tara said as she hurried over to the entrance... "Sir – you can't go in there..."

"My wife's in there!"

"I'm sorry - when did your wife die?"

"She didn't die – she went to go visit her mother – I need to find her!"

"Scott – we're going in..."

"Denise! Where are you?"

"Titus! I'm here!"

"I'm coming!" Titus yelled as he ran with Tara and the cameras following behind him...

"Denise!" he breathed as he pulled her up off the ground into his arms...

"Titus!" she cried... "Oh thank God!"

"What are you still doing here?"

"I fell asleep..."

"I'm Tara Rosenbloom..."

"I know who you are..." Denise beamed...

"Are you okay Maam?"

"I"m okay – my mother..."

"Your mother? Where's your mother?"

"She was here..."

"Your mother was here?" Titus asked...

"She pulled me down and protected me..."

"Oh wow... that's beautiful..." Tara said as she wiped her tears...

"Let's go – these zombies are crazy!" Titus said...

"Scott – did you get that?" Tara asked...

"We got it Tara..." Scott said as they hurried out the cemetery.

CHAPTER 4

"I can't wait to get upstairs and hug my wife and kids..." Chandler said out loud as he parked his car. When he got out and started walking to the entrance to his building, that's when he heard Jermoll calling...

"Sarge..."

"Naa – I know I must be tired..."

"Sarge!"

"Oh hell no!" Chandler snapped...

"Sarge – you gotta help me!"

"Yo – get the fuck outta here!" Chandler yelled as he walked towards the grass and bushes behind the parking lot with his gun drawn...

"That won't work..." Jermoll said...

"What the fuck are you talking about?" Chandler snapped. Chandler was unaware that the doorman followed him and was watching and listening...

"Sarge... I don't wanna be here..."

"So leave!" Chandler snapped...

"I can't leave... unless you crush my skull..."

"Why me? Why didn't you ask one a them?"

"They kept shooting... they wouldn't listen..."

"I'm not listening either..."

"Sarge! Just pick up that rock... make it quick... and I'll be gone..."

"I can't do it Jermoll..."

"Sarge... please..."

"I'ma turn around... I'ma go upstairs... I'ma kiss my wife... I'ma kiss my kids... and I'ma act like I didn't see you..." Chandler said as he turned to walk away... "Noooo!" Chandler yelled as he tried to stop the doorman but couldn't... Bam! Bam! Bam!

"Blake..." Chandler called on his radio...

"Yea Sarge?"

"We need a unit... and a body bag..."

"Where?"

"My parking lot..." Chandler sighed...

"Mr. Chandler..."

"Go inside... and stay there..."

"Yes Sir Mr. Chandler..." the doorman said as he walked back to the entrance of the complex and Chandler took out his cell phone...

"You good Sarge?' Blake asked as he hurried over to where Chandler was standing...

"I'm good..."

"Oh shit! What happened?"

27

"Looks to me like somebody took out a zombie..." Chandler laughed...

"You sure it's a zombie?"

"It's a zombie – look at the decomposer of the body..."

"You're right – I wonder what it was doing here?"

"Who knows?" Chandler answered as the ambulette pulled up...

"Hey Sarge – how many we got?"

"We got one..."

"Oh shit – I guess we don't have to worry about this one..." the tech laughed as he bagged Jermoll's body...

"We sure don't" Blake laughed...

"Okay – we got it – we'll get this over to the crematorium..." the tech said as he put Jermoll's body in the ambulette, closed the door, jumped in the driver's seat, and drove off...

"Okay Sarge – if you need me..."

"I know, I know..."

"Good night..."

"Good night..." Chandler said as he went upstairs...

"This is Della Crews, News 12 Connecticut. Earlier this evening, we were bringing you live coverage with Gwen Edwards in downtown Bridgeport. Zombies were spotted on McLevy Green and as officers were attempting to block the area, Gwen lost her connection due to technical issues. At the same time, we contacted the Landscaping Corporation, and Liam, President, issued the following statement:

"We are sorry to learn that our fertilizer is responsible for these recent incidents. As of today, we have stopped producing the fertilizer. All fertilizer has been removed from stores in Westchester County as well as Fairfield Counties. Anyone that still has fertilizer is encouraged to either reach out to the Landscaping Corporation directly to have it picked up and disposed of or to return it to the store where it was purchased for a full refund. Please - DO NOT throw the fertilizer in garbage cans..."

"I'm Della Crews, News 12 Connecticut. We'll continue to bring you updates..."

"Good morning Mrs. Osgood..." Bazil breathed as he kissed Beautiee awake..."
"Mmmm... good morning..." she breathed...
"What would you like for breakfast?" he asked as he began kissing her on her neck...
"I'd like dessert..." she breathed as she arched her back...
"Cumming right up..." he breathed and then he put his tongue in her mouth, climbed on top of her, and spread her legs... "Shit!"
"Is... that... your... phone?" she breathed between kisses...
"Mmmm hmmmm...."
"Answer it..."

29

"No..."

"It... could... be... important..."

"This is important..." he breathed as he eased himself inside her...

"Bazil... Huh..."

"Yes... Beautiee..." Bazil thrust his tongue in her mouth and started thrusting harder...

"Mmmm... Mmmm... Mmmm..."

"Mmmph... Mmmph... Mmmph..."

"Mmmm... Mmmm... Mmmm..."

"Mmmph... Mmmph... Mmmph..." Beautiee grabbed Bazil's ass, spread her legs, and pushed him in deeper...

"Bazil... Fuck... I'm cumming..."

"Cum for me..." he growled...

"Haah... Haah... Haah... Haaaaahhhh!"

"Uuugh! Uuugh! Uuugh! Uuuuggghhhh!"

"I needed that..." she breathed...

"I know..." he breathed as he kissed her neck...

"It's been so long since we've been able to fuck without being interrupted..."

"I know..." he breathed as he continued kissing her neck...

"I need to do this more often..."

"Mmmm... sounds good..." he breathed as he kissed her again... "Shit!"

"Answer it..."

"No..."

"Bazil..."

"No..."

"It could be the kids..."

"Okay..." Bazil said as he picked up the phone...

"Good morning..."

"Bazil – I've been trying to call you..."

"Do we have a court date?"

"Have you seen News 12?"

"Not since last night..."

"Turn on News 12..."

"Okay..." he said as he got up to turn on the television...

"This is Della Crews, News 12 Connecticut. Earlier this evening, we were bringing you live coverage with Gwen Edwards in downtown Bridgeport. Zombies were spotted on McLevy Green and as officers were attempting to block the area, Gwen lost her connection due to technical issues. At the same time, we contacted the Landscaping Corporation, and Liam, President, issued the following statement:

"We are sorry to learn that our fertilizer is responsible for these recent incidents. As of today, we have stopped producing the fertilizer. All fertilizer has been removed from stores in Westchester County as well as Fairfield Counties. Anyone that still has fertilizer is encouraged to either reach out to the Landscaping Corporation Corporation directly to have it picked up and disposed of or to return it to the store where it was purchased for a full refund. Please - DO NOT throw the fertilizer in garbage cans..."

"I'm Della Crews, News 12 Connecticut. We'll continue to bring you updates..."

"Is this for real?" Bazil asked...

"It's real..."

"Thank you..."

"You're welcome..."

"I don't believe it..." Beautiee said...

"Neither do I..."

"I can't wait to tell your parents..."

"We did it!" Bazil said as he pulled her up into his arms and kissed her...

"You did it..."

"Let's go have breakfast – then we'll go see the kids...

"Okay..."

CHAPTER 5

"Good morning..." Sam said as they walked in...

"Good morning..." they said in unison...

"The landscapers need to see you..."

"Okay – let's go see them now..." Bazil said as they walked outside and went around to the back of the building where they had grass, flowers, and bushes...

"Good morning..." Bazil said as they approached the landscapers...

"Good morning Mr. Osgood, good morning Mrs. Osgood..." the supervisor said...

"It looks good..." Beautiee said...

"Thank you Mrs. Osgood..." one of the landscapers said...

"Mr. Osgood – we have something to tell you..." the supervisor said...

"What's wrong?"

"It's good..."

"I don't understand..."

33

"We re-planted the bushes, we re-planted the flowers, we sprayed with Weed Killer... and nothing happened..."

What do you mean nothing happened?"

"The zombies didn't come back..."

"Ooohhh..." Beautiee said...

"I'm surprised it didn't kill the plants..." Sam said...

"Thank you..." Bazil said...

"You're welcome..."

"C'mon – let's go inside..." Bazil said as they walked back to the main entrance...

"I'm going to check on my wife – call me if you need me..." Sam said and then he headed towards his office. When they got in their office, Bazil pushed the door closed, locked it, and pulled Beautiee into a kiss...

"Mr. Osgood..." she breathed...

"Yes Mrs. Osgood?" he breathed as he kissed her neck...

"As much as I'm enjoying this..."

"Go on..." he breathed as he started kissing her down her chest...

"We need... to... get... to work..."

"I couldn't agree more..." he breathed as he picked her up, wrapped her legs around him, carried her over to the couch, lay her down, and lay on top of her...

"Bazil..." she whispered...

"Ssshhh..." he breathed and then he kissed her...

"Bazil..." she whispered again. Bazil covered her mouth with his and pushed his tongue in her mouth to keep her from talking and just as he started tonguing her down, the phone rang...

"Mmmm...." she moaned as she deliberately pulled him down and locked her legs behind him...

"Beautiee..." he breathed... "I need to get that..."

"I know..." she sighed as she unlocked her legs and he got up to answer the phone...

"Hello Liam..." Bazil answered as he put the phone on speaker...

"Hello Bazil – how'd you know it was me?"

"You came up on the caller ID..."

"I see..." he laughed...

"What else can I do for you?" Bazil asked...

"Oh – you got jokes..." Liam laughed...

"I'm sorry – I didn't mean to offend you..."

"Yes you did..." he laughed... "But since you asked – le'me answer your question..."

"Okay..."

"You know I was comin' for you – right?"

"Yes..."

"Well – I've decided I'm not going to do that..."

"Thank you..."

"It's not about you... not really..."

"Okay..."

"I've been testing our new fertilizer since you went to News 12..."

"You have?"

"Yes... and... I can't believe I'm saying this – this stays between us – you can't repeat what I'm about to tell you..."

"You have my word..."

"I'm serious!"

"As I said... you have my word..."

"Okay... so we killed two rats... a male... and a female..."

"Okay...."

"We buried them in the fertilizer..."

"Okay..."

"We watered it... and we waited..."

"What happened?"

"We had rats fuckin' in the lab!" he laughed...

"I'm glad you're laughing..." Bazil said as Beautiee's mouth dropped open...

"I wasn't laughing at first – I was comin' for your ass – but once I saw that – I couldn't – especially after you said what you said about your parents..."

"Yea..."

"I'm sorry you had to see that..."

"I'm not..."

"You weren't freaked out by seeing your parents fuckin'?'

"Is this conversation being recorded?"

"Bazil! How could you ask me that?"

"I'm sorry – it hasn't been easy – thank God for my wife..."

"You're a lucky man..."

"I am..."

"So... after we saw what we saw... we reached out to Pfizer and they referred us to Greenstone..."

"What's Greenstone?"

"A subsidiary of Pfizer..."

"The makers of Viagara?"

"I knew you'd get that..."

"Oh wow..."

"Our fertilizer is made with natural ingredients and it's plant-based so patients that use Viagra can use our product without any side effects – except the obvious one..." Bazil bust out laughing...

"What's so funny?"

"We were making a joke about that the other day – and now it's happening..." he laughed...

"We're working on the patent now – we just need to figure out how to turn it off..." Liam laughed...

"Turn it off?"

"We don't want men walking around with erections for 12 hours!" he laughed...

"I guess not..." Bazil laughed...

"We're working on Rise now – it should be available before the end of the year..."

"Rise? I like it!"

"Thank you Bazil..."

"You're welcome..."

"I have your word – right?"

"You have my word..." Bazil said as he hung up...

"Sam?" Bazil called on the intercom...

"Yes Bazil?"

"I need to see you..."

"I'll be right there..." Sam said as he hung up...

"Bazil – you gave your word!" Beautiee whispered...

"Yes Bazil?" Sam asked as he came in..."

"I need you to purchase 25 shares of Pfizer and 25 shares of the Landscaping Corporation..."

"Pfizer? The pharmaceutical company?"

"That's the one – and I want the shares to be owned by Osgood Publishing..."

"Okay..."

"I also want you to purchase 25 shares for Joselyn as well as yourself..."

"Hold on a minute..." Sam said as he pulled out his phone. Bazil watched Sam google the information and use the calculator... "Bazil – that's nearly two thousand dollars..."

"Okay..."

"We don't have two thousand dollars right now..." Bazil took out his checkbook and wrote Sam a check for two thousand dollars – payable to cash...

"Now you have two thousand dollars..."

"Umm... okay... thank you..."

"You're welcome – send Sheila in here..."

"Yes Sir!" Sam said as he hurried out the office...

"What's going on?" Joselyn asked...

Bazil needs me to run an errand – you're coming with me – Sheila – Bazil needs to see you..." Sam said as he took Joselyn by the hand and pulled her out the office...

"You wanted to see me?" Sheila asked as she came into our office...

"Yes I did – here's a check for one thousand dollars – I want you to go buy 25 shares of Pfizer and 25 shares of the Landscaping Corporation for yourself..."

"Would you like me to leave right now?"

"Sure – that's fine..."

"I'll see you tomorrow..." she said as she hurried out the door. Bazil picked up the phone and called Chandler...

"Hi Dad – everything alright?"

"Everything's fine – can you bring the kids down here?"

"Ummm... sure – but I don't get off for another half hour..."

"That's fine..."

"Okay Dad..." Chandler said as he hung up and called Starr...

"Hello Bazil..." Smalls said...

"Hello Smalls..."

"You good?"

"I'm good..."

"How can I help you?"

"I need you to purchase 25 shares of Pfizer and 25 shares of the Landscaping Corporation for me, my wife, my children... and yourself..."

"Okay – how much are they?"

"$18 per share..."

"Okay... $18 per share... 25 shares each... $7,000?"

"No – Starr will be taken care of..."

"$6,000?"

"That's right..."

"I'm on it!" Smalls said as he hurried off the phone..."

"Bazil – you good?" Troy asked...

"I'm good – I need you and Keisha to come down here..."

"Everything's good?"

"Everything's good...

"We're on our way..."

"What's wrong?" Keisha asked...

"Nothing..." Troy answered as he headed to our office...

"Mrs. Osgood?"

"Yes Mr. Osgood?" she answered as he got up from behind the desk and went to lock the door. After he locked the door he came over to the couch and sat down beside Beautiee...

"We have 30 minutes..." he breathed as he pushed her down on the couch and lay down on top of her.

CHAPTER 6

"Hi Mommy!" Starr answered...

"Hi Starr!" Sky beamed...

"Sky! Oh my God! You got so big! Everybody come say hi to Sky!" All the kids came running...

"Hi Sky!" Hi Starr Mommy! Hi Sky Daddy! Hi Grandpa!" they all said and then they ran back in the room to play...

"Hi Starr!" Wayne said...

"Hi Dad..."

"We're thinking of coming to see you next week – I wanted to surprise you but Wayne reminded me about Chandler's schedule..." Mary said...

"Chandler doesn't really have a schedule..." Starr laughed...

"That's what I told her..." Wayne said...

"I can't wait to see you..." Mary said...

"Mommy..."

"What's wrong?"

"I wish I could see you Mommy..."

"Why can't you?"

"Maybe you can come next month..." Starr sighed...

"Mary – give me the phone..."

"Here..."

"Starr – what's going on?" Wayne asked...

"You won't believe me..."

"Try me..."

"Okay... so... Daddy and Beautiee had to go to school for Jay because he drew a picture..."

"Was it a parent-teacher conference?"

"Kinda..."

"Starr... tell me..."

"Jay drew a picture of Daddy and Beautiee in bed..."

"Oh my God – please don't tell me he got in trouble for that!" Mary snapped...

"No Mommy..."

"Mary – let her finish..."

"Jay drew a picture of monsters on the grass so the teacher thought Jay was scared..."

"Oh okay – I get it – maybe they should close their door..." Mary said...

"No Mommy – Jay saw something in the backyard..."

"Oh my God! Somebody tried to break in?"

"No..." she answered as she started crying...

"Starr... please don't cry..." Wayne said as he started tearing up...

"Something's going on with your father – right?" Mary asked...

"Yea..."

"What's going on Starr? Is your father in danger?" Wayne asked...

"I can't explain it..."

"Starr – you can trust me – you know that – right?"

"I guess..."

"Tell me..."

"Okay... so... Daddy's parents were in the backyard..."

"His parents? That's ridiculous – his parents are dead!" Mary snapped...

"Mommy!"

"Mary – let her finish!"

"They came to ask for his help... and to warn him..."

"What do they need help with?"

"They needed Daddy to tell the Landscaping Corporation to stop producing their fertilizer because... don't laugh at me..."

"Starr – nobody's laughing at you..."

"The fertilizer wakes up the dead... and"

"What Starr?"

"They can't stop having sex..."

"Aaaahaaaa! Aaaahaaaa!" Mary laughed...

"Mary! Stop it!" Wayne snapped...

"I can't help it!" she laughed... Zombies? Fuckin Zombies? Aaaahaaaa!"

"I knew I shouldn'tve told you..." Starr said and then she hung up...

43

"Mary! Why would you do that to her?"

"Wayne – please don't tell me you believe what she said!" Mary laughed...

"Something's going on – and instead of laughing at her – maybe you should look into it..." Wayne said as he got up from the table and went into the bedroom...

"Daddy mad at Mommy?" Sky asked with tears in her eyes as she came in...

"Come here Sky..." Wayne said as he picked her up and held her... "Daddy's not mad at Mommy..."

"But you were yelling..."

"Yes I was... and I'm sorry..."

"Say sorry to Mommy..." Sky said as she jumped down off of Wayne's lap and went back in her room. Wayne opened his laptop, googled News 12 Connecticut, and watched Bazil's interview...

"Good evening – I'm Gwen Edwards, Reporter, News 12 Connecticut. Tonight I'm here with Bazil Osgood, President and CEO of Osgood Publishing to bring you an exclusive – Go ahead Mr. Osgood...

"Earlier this week, my son was woken out of his sleep by noise in my backyard...

"Was there a break in?"

"I looked out the window... and I saw... zombies..."

"Mr. Osgood – is this some type of publicity stunt?"

"Ms. Edwards – I wouldn't be sitting here with Sergeant Corbett of Bridgeport, Sergeant Hurley of Milford, my wife, or my neighbors if I were trying to get publicity – unless I was being arrested..."

"I'm sorry – you said you saw zombies..."

"Yes – I saw them out the window..."

"How did they get in your backyard?"

"They came up through the grass..."

"What where they doing there?"

"Once I went out into the backyard... I realized the zombies were my parents..."

"Your parents?"

"My parents were there to ask for my help... and to warn me..."

"What do your parents need your help with?"

"My parents need you to contact the Landscaping Corporation and tell them they need to stop producing their new fertilizer..."

"Why would your parents... wait a minute – are you saying this new fertilizer wakes up the dead?"

"Once you water your plants, there's an ingredient in the fertilizer and once that gets absorbed into the soil... it wakes up the dead... and..."

"What Mr. Osgood?"

"The zombies aren't able to control their sexual urges..."

"Oh my God..."

"We've started getting reports from residents in Milford claiming that they've seen zombies having sex in their backyard..." Sergeant Hurley said...

"I also took a couple of reports today in Bridgeport claiming the same thing..." Chandler said

"We didn't actually see any zombies – but my husband could tell something went down in our backyard..."

"What's your name Maam?"

"I'm Keisha Cochran – this is my husband, Troy..."

"Mr. Cochran – what did you see when you went in your backyard?"

"It looked like something came up out the dirt..."

"Have you been in your backyard since?"
"No..."

"Mr. Osgood – you said your parents were there to ask for your help – and to warn you..."

"Yes..."

"What was the warning?"

"Zombies are coming..."

"I have a backyard – I like to entertain – do I need to be afraid?"

"They only come out at night – but after what I saw in Troy's backyard... you won't want to entertain..."

"This is Gwen Edwards, Reporter, News 12 Connecticut and you're watching an exclusive interview where we've just learned Erotic

Zombies have been observed by residents here in Fairfield County..."

"Oh my God..." he said out loud as he watched the 2nd story...

"This is Della Crews, News 12 Connecticut. Earlier this evening, the Osgoods were spotted going into the Holiday Inn, where we were able to get a few comments from Mrs. Osgood..."

"Mrs. Osgood – have you seen the zombies? We're you scared?"

"Yes, I've seen his parents in our backyard..."

"Were you scared?"

"I'm not afraid of his parents..."

"Were they having sex when you saw them?"

"Yes they were..."

"Uh uh! Get these cameras away from these kids!"

"What's that? Hang on...we've just been notified that Erotic Zombies have been spotted at McLevy Green, downtown Bridgeport. Gwen Edwards is live on the scene – Gwen – what can you tell us?"

"Della – it's crazy – as you can see behind me – officers are attempting to block the area by taping it off as some of the officers are fighting off the zombies..."

"Did you say fighting? The officers are actually fighting?"

"The officers are attempting to block the zombies from leaving and the zombies are attempting to push back – oh shit..."

"Gwen? Gwen are you there? We've lost contact – we'll be back momentarily – we'll keep you posted..."

After Wayne was done watching, he closed his laptop, picked it up, and carried it into the kitchen... "You have something you wanna say to me?" Mary asked...

"I have something I need to show you..." he answered as he put his laptop on the table, opened it, and played the 1st story for Mary...

"Oh my God... she was telling the truth... Wayne... I'm so sorry..."

"I'm not the one you need to apologize to..." Wayne said as he left Mary in the kitchen and went back to the bedroom. Mary watched the 2nd story, closed the laptop, and picked up her phone to call Starr...

"Voice mail – okay – here goes... Starr... I'm sorry... please call me..." Starr picked up her phone, rolled her eyes, and threw it down on the dresser.

"Daddy! Chandler! Uncle Chandler!" they squealed when they saw him...

"Y'all ready?"

"I'm ready!" Chandler Jr. squealed...

"You don't even know where we're going..." Chandler laughed...

"Yes I do!"

"Where we goin'?"

"Outside!"

"Yeeaaa!" they all squealed...

"I'll be right back..." he said and then he went to the bedroom... "Starr?"

"Hi Chandler..." she sighed...

"Uh uh – what happened?"

"I did something stupid..." she sighed as Chandler puller her into a hug and held her...

"What happened?"

"Please don't be mad at me..."

"Mad at you for what?"

'Mommy called..."

49

"You told her?"

"Yea..."

"Okay..."

"You're not mad?"

"No Starr... I'm not mad..."

"She laughed at me..." Starr said as she started crying...

"Uh uh... stop that..." Chandler said and then he kissed her...

"But Chandler..." Chandler pulled her into a deep kiss, put his tongue in her mouth, and held her as he tongued her down...

"Mmmm..." she moaned...

"Let's go..." Chandler said as he took her by the hand and led her into the living room...

"We ready!" they all said in unison...

"Let's go!" Chandler said as they left and Mary left another message on Starr's phone...

"Bazil – you in there?" Troy asked as he knocked...

"Hold on..." Bazil answered as he got up to unlock the door...

"Hey..." Keisha said as she came into the office and sat down on the couch... "This is nice!"

"Thank you – Joselyn had our office re-decorated..."

"Oh that's nice..."

"Bazil – what's going on?" Troy asked...

"I'm waiting for Chandler..."

"Oh shit – this must be serious..."

"It is..."

"Hey Dad..." Chandler said as he walked in... "Hey Troy, Keisha..."

"Hey Chan..." Keisha said... "Where are the kids?"

"They're coming in with Starr..."

"Hi Daddy, Hi Beautiee..." Starr said as she came in with the kids...

"Mommy!" Amina said as she ran to Keisha... "Are we going home now?"

"We'll go home in a little while..." Troy answered...

"Okay Chandler – I need you to do something for me..." Bazil said as he took out his checkbook and started writing...

"Okay – watcha need?"

"I need you to take this check, deposit it, and then buy 25 shares of Pfizer and 25 shares of the Landscaping Corporation for you, Starr, and each of my grandchildren..."

"Pfizer Pharmaceuticals?"

"Yes..."

"Okay..." Chandler said as he put the check in his pocket...

"Troy – I need you to do something for me too..." Bazil said as he wrote another check...

"Okay..."

"I need you to take this check, deposit it, and buy 25 shares of Pfizer and 25 shares of the Landscaping Corporation for you, Keisha, and Amina..."

"Thank you..." Troy said...

"You're welcome..."

51

"You feelin' alright Bazil?" Keisha laughed...

"Yes Keisha – I'm fine..." Bazil laughed...

"Daddy – I need to talk to you..." Starr said...

"We'll talk later..." he said as he got up... "C'mon – I'll show you around..." Bazil said as they all left the office and went down the hall...

"Oh my God! They're so cute!" Shadajah said when she saw them...

"Thank you!" they all said in unison...

"Shadajah, this is my daughter Starr, her husband Chandler, and their children Chelsea, Kalliyah, and Chandler...

"You're pretty..." Shadajah told Starr...

"Thank you..."

"These are our children Jay, Joseph, and Joy..."

"Hi Shadajah..." Joy said...

"These are our best friends Troy and Keisha, and this is their daughter Amina..."

"Hi..." Amina said...

"Look at you actin' all bashful!" Troy laughed...

"Shadajah works here..." Beautiee said...

"I wanna work here too!" Jay said...

"Me too!" Joseph said...

"I'm hungry!" Joy said...

"C'mon – we'll go to the cafeteria..." Bazil said as they continued walking down the hall towards the cafeteria...

"Hi!" A'Licia greeted...

"This is A'Licia – she works here too..." Beautiee said...

"Hi – I gotta go to the bathroom – excuse me..." she said as she hurried down the hall..."

"Oooh look!" Jay squealed as he saw the cafeteria and started running...

"Slow down!" Chandler yelled to no avail...

"I want juice"

"I want jello!"

"I want ice cream!"

"I want pizza!"

"Me too!"

"Is the pizza any good here?" Chandler asked...

"It's okay – but when I eat here, I usually get a burger..." Bazil answered...

"Beautiee – whatchu get?" Keisha asked...

"Coffee..." she laughed...

"Damn – watchu do when you get hungry?"

"We go out..." she answered as Bazil took her hand and they looked at each other...

"Aiight – pizza and burgers!" Troy said...

"Yeeaaa!" the kids squealed as they ran to sit at the table and Chandler, Starr, Keisha, and Troy followed...

"Mr. Osgood – you brought your family – how nice!" the cook said...

"Thank you..."

"Since they want pizza, le'me make them a couple a fresh ones..." he said as he put two pies in the oven...

"How long will that take?" Beautiee asked...

"About 5 minutes..."

'We'll have burgers..." Bazil said...

"How many?"

"Six..."

"Everything?"

"Everything..."

"Fries?"

"Fries..."

"Henney?" Bazil and Beautiee looked at him, looked at each other, and bust out laughing...

"That was a good one Jack..." Bazil laughed...

"It would be even better if you sold it..." Jack laughed as he put their burgers on the grill and Beautiee went to get six ginger ales and put them on the table...

"Thanks!" Chandler said...

"You're welcome..." Beautiee said as she left to get some Capri sun's for the kids and put them on the table...

"Thank you!" they all said in unison...

"You're welcome – don't open them until after you eat..."

"Pizza's done – you want me to bring it to the table?"

"We got it – thanks Jack..." Bazil said as he picked up one tray, Beautiee picked up the other, and they brought the pizza to the table...

"Thank you!" they all squealed...

"I'ma get some napkins and plates – I'll be right back..." she said. Starr got up to follow her...

"Beautiee – I need to talk to you..." she whispered...

"We'll talk later..." Beautiee said and then she took the plates and napkins to the table...

"Burgers are ready!" Jack yelled...

"We'll be right there..." Bazil said as we both went over to get plates...

"Y'all need help?" Troy asked...

"We got it..." Beautiee said as they put the plates in front of them and then they went to get their food, came back to the table, and sat down with them...

"I need to talk to you..." Starr said...

"Starr..." Chandler interrupted...

"Chandler... please..."

"Okay..." he sighed as he shook his head...

"What's wrong Starr?" Bazil asked...

"Please don't be mad..."

"Depends on what you tell me..."

"Mommy called..."

"That's nice – how's she doing?"

"They're fine – they wanted to come visit next week but..."

"You told her..."

"Yea..."

"Is that what has you so bummed out?" Beautiee asked...

"She laughed at me..."

"Oh Starr... I'm sorry..." Beautiee said as she squeezed her hand...

"You're not mad?"

"I'm mad..." Keisha said...

"Keisha!" Troy exclaimed...

"I'm mad 'cause she laughin' – this shit ain't funny!"

"Ooohhh... Mommy!" Amina said...

"Mind your business!" Keisha snapped and Amina looked away...

"I told her don't worry about it..." Chandler said...

"It's all over the news – I'm surprised they didn't call you sooner..." Beautiee said...

"They don't have News 12 up there in Canada..." Bazil said...

"You're right – I forgot..."

"My sister is getting so big..." Starr said...

"Did you talk to Wayne?" Chandler asked...

"Yea..."

"How's he doing?"

"He's fine..." she sighed...

"They can come down here when this is over..." Chandler said...

"What if it's never over?"

"It'll be over soon... I promise..." Bazil said as he picked up her hand and kissed it...

"Y'all finished?" Troy asked the kids...

"Yeesss..." they all answered in unison...

"Was it good?"

"Yeesss..." they all answered again...

"Okay – we finished – and our food was good too..." Troy laughed...

"C'mon – let's go..." Bazil said as he got up...

"Have a good day!" Jack beamed as we were leaving...

"Thank you – you too..." Beautiee said as they left the cafeteria and Mary left another voicemail...

CHAPTER 8

"She's not answering..." Mary sighed...

"What'd you expect?" Wayne asked...

"I know... I'm sorry..."

"Stop fighting!" Sky said...

"We're not fighting Sky..." Wayne said...

"I never should've laughed at her..."

"She'll forgive you..."

"I wish we could go see her..."

"So let's go then..."

"You mean it?"

"Of course I do..." Wayne said as he pulled Mary up out the chair and held her...

"What about what Starr said?"

"She needs us... I heard it in her voice..."

"So we're going?"

"I already bought the tickets..."

"Oh Wayne... I love you..."

"I love you too..."

"Me too!" Sky squealed as she tugged on Wayne's robe and he picked her up...

"Hey Chandler, Starr – where y'all been?" Charles asked...

"We've been out and about..." Chandler answered as they came off the elevator...

"Uncle Charles! Auntie Theresa! Charles!" they squealed when they saw them. Lil' Charles came running towards the kids with his arms wide open and they all hugged each other...

"They are so cute..." Theresa laughed as Chandler opened the door and they all went inside...

"Mommy – we goin' home – right?" Amina asked...

"Yes Amina..." Keisha sighed...

"No Amina – I don't want you to go home..." Lil' Charles whined...

"I'll stay..." Amina said...

"You sure?" Keisha asked...

"Ummm..."

"Girl – go on and play..." Troy laughed...

"Okay!" they squealed as they ran down the hall...

"I can't believe they were right downstairs..." Charles said...

"Chandler – you weren't scared?" Theresa asked...

"Ain't no need in bein' scared of a dead man..." Chandler answered...

"I wonder what it was doing here though?" Charles asked...

59

"Maybe it knew somebody here..." Chandler answered...

"Oh shit – I just thought of something – what if it used to live here?!" Theresa exclaimed...

"Naaa... these units been full for a while..." Chandler said...

"I'll be glad when this is over – I need Lil' Charles to go back to school..." Charles said...

"Send him back if you want..." Bazil said...

"Naaa... I can't answer all those questions..."

"You won't have to – it's been all over News 12..." Bazil said...

"I'm sure we're not the only ones that pulled their kids out of school..." Beautiee said...

"Yes – but we're the only ones they've seen on tv..." Charles said...

"I don't think you have anything to worry about..." Bazil said...

"They might ask Lil' Charles about the other kids..."

"They might..."

"I'll just let Lil' Charles stay home until all the kids go back..."

"Sounds good..."

"I'll be right back..." Starr said as she got up from the table, went into the bedroom, picked up her phone, sat on the bed, and played her messages...

"Starr... I'm sorry... please call me..."

"You should've thought about that before you laughed at me..." she said as she listened to the second message...

"Starr... I'm worried about you... please call me back..."

"Oh now you're worried..." she laughed as she played the third message...

"Starr – we're on our way – we'll be there tomorrow afternoon..."

"Starr?"

"Yes Chandler?"

"Come here..." Starr got up off the bed, went over to Chandler, and kissed him... "You okay?"

"I'm fine..." she said as she wrapped her arms around his neck...

"You fine alright..." Chandler said as he pushed her back against the door and locked it...

"Chandler..." she whispered as he started kissing her neck...

"I'm glad you're feeling better..." he breathed in her ear...

"Chandler..."

"Ssshhh..." he said and then he kissed her...

"I need to tell you something..."

"Okay... what?"

"Mommy's coming..."

"When?"

"Tomorrow..."

"C'mon – let's go..." Chandler said as he opened the door, took Starr by the hand, and led her back into the living room...

"There's my girl..." Bazil said...

"Mary and Wayne will be here tomorrow..." Chandler said...

"How long are they staying?" Beautiee asked...

"Mommy didn't say..." Starr answered...

"We gotta get going – Amina you stayin'?" Keisha asked. Amina came running...

"I wanna go home!"

"Okay – get your stuff..." Troy said...

"Daddy – can we go home?" Jay asked...

"Not yet..." Bazil sighed. Jay didn't say anything – he just started crying...

"Why you cryin' Jay?" Joseph asked as he started crying too...

"Come here..." Beautiee said with my arms stretched out and they both ran to her... "I know this is hard..." she said as she fought back tears... "But you'll go home soon...

"We don't have to live here?" Joseph asked...

"No son... you're just on vacation – that's why you're not going to school..."

"We're on vacation?" Joy asked...

"Yes..." Beautiee answered...

"Oh – okay... c'mon Jay – c'mon Joseph..."

"We need to go home now..." Bazil said...

"Daddy – why can't you stay here and be on vacation with us?" Joy asked...

62

"Because they have to work — right Daddy?" Jay asked...

"Yes Jay — we have to work — but we'll be back tomorrow..."

"I love you Mommy..." Joy said as she hugged Beautiee really tight...

"I love you too..." Beautiee said as she choked back tears...

I love you Daddy..." Joy said as she hugged Bazil...

"I love you too..."

"I love my big boys..." Beautiee said as she hugged them..."

"We love you too Mommy..."

"Come give Daddy hugs..." Bazil said...

"We love you Daddy..."

"I love you too — we'll see you tomorrow..." we said as we got up to leave...

"Good night..." Bazil said as we left...

"Good night y'all..." Troy said as they came out behind us with Amina...

"Mommy — can I come back tomorrow?" Amina asked...

"Yes Amina..." Keisha sighed as we all went towards the elevator...

When they got home Beautiee couldn't hold it in any longer... "Beautiee..." Bazil said as he pulled her into a hug and she burst into tears... "I know..." he said as he kissed her...

"That just broke my heart..." she cried...

"I know... I'm sorry..."

"It's not your fault..."

"It'll be over soon..."

"I hope so..." she said as they went upstairs. When she got in the bedroom, she took off her clothes, walked into the bathroom, turned on the shower, and got in...

"May I join you?" Bazil asked, smiling at her mischievously...

"You better..."

CHAPTER 9

"I'm Scott McGee, Anchor and Managing Editor, News 12 Yonkers. We interrupt our regularly scheduled programming to bring you this update. We now go live to Samantha Crawford. Go ahead Samantha..."

"Scott – I'm standing near Glenn Island in New Rochelle – can you see what's going on behind me?"

"My God – what are they doing?"

"It's exactly what you think it is Scott – the zombies are running around, frolicking, and having sex – and if you can see over to the right – some of the zombies are engaged in a group orgy..."

"Samantha – I don't see the police – are they on the scene?"

"Scott – the police are on the scene – unfortunately they can't get close enough to barricade the area – hold on a second..."

"Samantha? Samantha - are you there?"

"I'm here Scott..."

"Did you I just hear gun shots?"

"Yes Scott – unfortunately the bullets aren't having an effect..."

"Thank you Samantha. I'm Scott McGee and you're watching News 12 Westchester. At this time, residents are being warned and urged to stay away from all parks and cemeteries until we can get this under control. News 12 Westchester will continue to bring you updates. We now return to our regularly scheduled programming..."

"I'm Della crews, Anchor, News 12 Connecticut. We interrupt our regularly scheduled programming to bring you this update. We now go live to Marissa Alter. Go ahead Melissa..."

"Della – I'm standing here with Brooke Bethea. We're at the New Stratford Motor Inn in Stratford, which is directly across the street from St. Michael's Cemetery – go ahead Brooke – tell us what you saw..."

"Oh my God – I came out my room to get some ice – I heard this moaning – at first I thought it was people in the room next door because these walls are paper thin – so after I got my ice I was going back to my room and I looked across the street and let me tell you..."

"Go ahead Brooke..."

"They we're going crazy! I took my phone out to record it and I was like – what the fuck are they doing?"

"What were they doing?"

"They were running all around the cemetery, knocking over tombstones, and fuckin'! – Oh – 'xcuse my language..."

"That's okay – Della – I'm crossing the street and moving closer to the cemetery – can you see what's going on in there?"

"I sure can – if it wasn't for the gate, they might be in the street. I'm Della Crews, News 12 Connecticut. At this time, residents are being warned and urged to stay away from all parks and cemeteries until further notice. News 12 will continue to bring you updates. We now return to our regularly scheduled programming..."

"BAAZZZIIILLLL!!"

"Oh shit!" Bazil exclaimed as he jumped up out the bed and ran downstairs with Beautiee running behind him. They ran into the kitchen, opened the French doors, and hurried into the backyard... "Dad – I'm here..."

"He's coming..." Lydia said...

"Come with me!" Beautiee said as she ran over to the shed and snatched the door open...

"He'll find us in here!" Lydia yelled...

"Trust me!" Beautiee yelled as she moved the lawnmower over to the side...

"Beautiee – what are you doing?" Bazil asked...

"Help me move the table..." she said as she started moving the chairs...

"Beautiee – we don' have time..."

"Dammit – I said move the table!" Bazil moved the table to the side... "Mom – Dad – get in the corner!" We hurried to the corner without question and stood there... "Bazil – put the table back over there..." Bazil did as he was told... "Now – put the lawnmower in front of the table..."

"What now?" Bazil asked...

"We wait..." Beautiee whispered...

"Beautiee – what are you up to?"

"Shh!" Bazil stood beside her and stayed quiet... "Here..." she whispered as she handed him the spade...

"What the hell?" Bazil whispered. Beautiee didn't bother answering him. We didn't have to wait long...

"Lydia..." Clayton called out...

"Oh God – he's here..." Lydia whispered as she clung to me behind the table...

"Lydia..." he called out again. Bazil held up the spade, ready to swing and Clayton snatched the door open...

"How sweet – you brought the family..." Clayton said as he came inside the shed and Bazil swung the spade...

"LISTEN TO ME!" Clayton growled as he caught the spade in his hand and snatched it from Bazil... "IF YOU MOVE – I'LL RIP YOUR FATHER'S HEAD OFF HIS NECK AND SMASH

HIS SKULL IN FRONT OF YOU..." and then he threw the spade down in front of them...

"Mi Lydia..." he said as he moved closer to Bazil's parents... "All you have to do is come with me... and this will all be over..." he said as he extended his hand...

"NEVER!" she screamed...

"Never say never..." Clayton said as he picked up the lawnmower, threw it to the side, picked up the table, threw it over, and Bazil picked up the spade...

"Mi Lydia..." Clayton whispered as he went to reach for her and I stepped in front of her...

"YOU'LL NEVER TAKE MY WIFE!" I growled...

"TRY AND STOP ME!" Clayton growled as he lunged for me and grabbed me. Beautiee snatched Lydia from behind us and pulled her away as we fought...

"YOU CAN'T KILL ME AGAIN!" Clayton laughed as we continued fighting and Clayton pinned me down... "FIRST... I'M GOING TO SMASH YOUR SKULL IN FRONT OF YOUR SON..." he growled as Beautiee grabbed the bottle of Weed Killer... "AND THEN... I'M GOING TO TAKE YOUR WIFE AND SHE'LL BE MINE THROUGH ETERNITY..." he growled as Beautiee started spraying... "AAAAGGGHHH!" he yelled as he let go of me and rubbed his eyes as Beautiee kept on spraying. I pushed Clayton off of me and yelled, "BAZIL! THE SPADE!" Bazil swung the spade

69

and cracked Clayton's skull as he fell to the ground... "UUUGH! UUUGH! UUUGH!" Bazil grunted as he continued swinging and I got up off the ground ... "Son... it's over..." I said as I touched Bazil on the shoulder. Bazil dropped the spade, I grabbed him, and he broke down in my arms...

"Beautiee... thank you..." Lydia said as they hugged each other...

"You're welcome..."

"How did you know?"

"Our landscapers told us..."

"Mom..." Bazil said as he came over and hugged his mother...

"Dad..." Beautiee said as she came to hug me...

"I knew I was right about you..."

"BAZIL!" Lydia said as she ran to me...

"MI LYDIA..." I breathed as I pulled her into a kiss...

"Is it really over?" Bazil asked...

"Yes... it's over..." I answered as I bent down and started pulling Clayton's body...

"Dad – what are you doing?"

"Finishing what your wife started..." I answered as I continued pulling Clayton's body out of the shed and into the backyard...

"Bazil... we have to go..." Lydia said...

"I'm coming..." I said as I went to stand beside her and took her hand...

"We have to go before the sun comes up... or we'll be lying in the grass like Clayton..." I said...

"I love you..." Bazil said...

"We love you too..." we said and then we went back down into the hole we came up out of...

"Beautiee..." Bazil whispered as went over to her, picked her up, and spun her around...

"We did it!" Beautiee said as he put her down...

"I love you so much..." he said as he held her face in his hands and kissed her...

"I love you too..."

"Let's go upstairs..." he said as he pulled her by the hand, led her into the kitchen, and she tripped over the ledge...

"I gotchu..." he laughed as he caught her...

"The kids can come home tomorrow..."

"Yes... they can..."

"But tonight it's just the two of us..."

"Yes... it is..."

"And I don't have to be quiet..." she said as he started kissing her on her neck...

"No... you don't..." he breathed in her ear...

"So... I want you to take me upstairs..."

"Okay..." he breathed as he kissed her...

"Make love to me..."

"Okay..." he breathed as he kissed her again...

"And make me cum so hard... I scream..."

"As you wish..." Bazil breathed as he picked her up in his arms, she wrapped her arms

71

around his neck, and he carried her upstairs to the bedroom...

"Bazil! Yes! Fuck me!" she screamed...

"Is this what you want? Huh?"

"Yes! Fuck me! Yes!" she screamed again as she braced herself against the headboard...

"CUM FOR ME!" Bazil growled as he grabbed her hair, pulled it, and smacked her ass...

"BAAZZZIIILLLL!! I'M CUMMING!! AAAAGGGGHHHHH!!"

"UGGHH!! UGGHH!! UGGHH!! UGGHH!! UUUUGGGGHHHHH!!"

"FUCK!" she breathed as she fell down on her stomach and Bazil fell down on top of her...

"Is that what you wanted?" he breathed in her ear as he started thrusting again...

"Yeeesss..."

"Don't move..."

"I won't..." she breathed as Bazil moved her arms up and continued thrusting... "Bazil... Huh..."

"Beautiee... Fuck..."

"Harder..."

"Are you sure?"

"Yeeesss...." she moaned...

"Uuugh... Uuugh... Uuugh..." Bazil moaned as her head hit the headboard with each thrust...

"Bazil... I'm cumming again..." Bazil quickened his pace and pushed himself up as he fucked her deeper... "Aaahh! Aaahh! Aaahh! Aaahh! AAAAAHHHH!"

Uuugh! Uuugh! Uuugh! Uuugh! Uuuuuuggghhhh!"

"I don't wanna move..." she panted. Bazil got up off her, turned her over on her back, spread her legs, lay on top of her, and was right back inside her... "It's been so long..."

"I know..." he breathed as he kissed her...

"We used to fuck like this all the time..."

"I know..." he breathed as he kissed her again...

"I miss this..."

"Me too..."

"It's going to be hard to be quiet again..."

"You're never quiet..." Bazil laughed and then he kissed her again...

"Okay... I'm not quiet... but I don't scream..." she laughed...

"That's because I put my tongue in your mouth so you can't..." he laughed...

"I wish we could do this more..."

"We'll come up with something..." he breathed and then he kissed her again...

"Bazil..."

"Yes... Beautiee..."

"I wanna write this story..." Bazil got off of her, lay beside her, and propped his head up on his elbow...

"Really?"

"Yes..."

"Why?"

"Because I want to honor your parents..."

"I love you so much..." he breathed and then he kissed her hard...

"I love you too... but I have to be honest..."

"Okay... tell me..."

"I want to honor your parents... I want to tell their story our way... and I want to get it copyright protected before anyone else can profit from it..."

"I love you..." he breathed and then he kissed he again...

"Mmmmm... is that a yes?"

"Yeesss..." he breathed as he got on top of her, spread her legs, eased himself inside her, covered her mouth with his, and started thrusting...

"Mmmm... Mmmm... Mmmm... Mmmm..."

"Mmmph... Mmmph... Mmmph... Mmmph..."

CHAPTER 10

"Good morning Mrs. Osgood..." Bazil breathed as he kissed Beautiee awake...

"Good morning..." she breathed as she stretched and arched her back...

"Mmmm... that gives me an idea..." he said as he got on top of her and slid down between her legs...

"Bazil... don't..." Bazil stopped and came back up between her legs...

"Ohh... you want some more dick..." he breathed as he kissed her...

"Bazil... get up..."

"What's wrong?"

"I gotta go!" she answered as she jumped up, ran into the bathroom, and hurled last night's dinner into the toilet...

"Beautiee? Are you okay?" he asked as he came running into the bathroom...

"I think so..."

"You sure?"

"Bazil..."

"Yes Beautiee?"

"Open that drawer..."

"Okay – you have vagisil, toothpaste, Tylenol and... a pregnancy test?"

"Yes Bazil..."

"Beautiee – when did you..."

"Remember we order two pregnancy tests before we went on our second honeymoon?"

"Oh my God..."

"Open it..." she smiled as Bazil tore into the box like a kid at Christmas....

"Here!"

"Thanks..." she laughed...

"You need me to leave?"

"No – stay..."

"Okay – can I watch?"

"Yes Bazil..." she laughed... "You can watch..." she laughed again as she sat down on the toilet, spread her legs, and peed...

"Oh my God – give it to me!" he squealed...

"Wait a minute!" she laughed as she got up and placed the pregnancy test on the sink. Bazil and Beautiee stood there holding each other tight as they both bent down to look at the results...

"Beautiee..." Bazil whispered as he started crying...

"We're gonna have another baby..." Beautiee said as she started crying too...

"I love you..."

"I love you too..." she said as they started kissing profusely...

76

"Let's take a shower..."

"Okay..." Bazil turned on the water, stepped inside, and extended his hand for her to take, and she stepped into the shower...

"Hello Baby..." Bazil said as he started rubbing her stomach...

"Lydia..."

"Lydia?"

"Yes..."

"Hi Lydia..." Bazil said as he pushed her back against the shower stall and kissed his way down...

"Bazil?" Beautiee yawned... "Bazil? Where are you? Hmmm – maybe he's downstairs making coffee..." she said out loud as she got out of bed, put on her robe and slippers, and went downstairs... "Okay – I guess you're not making coffee..." she sighed when she went into the kitchen, took two cups out the cabinet, and started making coffee... "What the hell is he doing out there?" she asked out loud as she went over to the French doors and looked outside. Bazil had the bottle of Weed Killer in one hand and was spraying all around the pool area with the other. When he got to the area in front of the shed he stopped for a few moments, and then he sprayed the area where we came up through the dirt. After he was done, he went back in the shed, came out with the spade, and began chopping at Clayton's body... "Bazil?"

"Beautiee – go back inside..." She didn't listen to him – instead she went outside and walked past him... "Beautiee – what are you doing?"

"I'm making coffee..." she answered as she went in the shed, took a lawn bag down from the shelf, and came back outside...

"I thought you said you were making coffee?"

"I am..." she answered as she dropped the lawn bag on Clayton's body. Beautiee went back into the kitchen and finished making the coffee as Bazil put Clayton's body in the lawn bag, tied it, and put it in the garbage bin...

"Mmmm... smells good..." he said as he came inside...

"It is..." she said as she handed him a cup of coffee and they went to sit down at the table... "What'd you do with the body?"

"I put it in the garbage..."

"Did you put the garbage out?"

"Not yet..."

"I can't believe it's over..."

"Neither can I..."

"I can't believe we're having another baby..."

"I love you..."

"I love you too..."

"What would you like to do first?"

"I'd like to go to News 12..."

"Really?"

"Yea..."

"You're happy..."

"Yea..."

"So am I..."

"After we go to News 12, I want to go tell our kids they can come home... and then I want to bring them home..."

"Okay..."

"I want to sound-proof our room..."

"Okay..."

"I want to re-decorate Joy's room..."

"Okay..."

"I want to have my cover designer design a cover for the book about your parents..."

"Okay..." Bazil laughed...

"And I want to finish what I started in the living room the other night..." Bazil got up from the table, went over to her, and pulled her into a kiss... "Mmmm..."

"I'm going to ask you again..." he breathed in her ear... "What..." he said as he kissed her mouth... "Do..." he said as he kissed her left nipple... "You" he said as he kissed her right nipple... "Want..." he said as he kissed her stomach... "To..." he said as he spread her lips... "Do..." he said as he flicked her clit with his tongue... "First..." he said as he pulled her body towards him and started sucking...

"Bazil... Huh... Huh... Huh..."

"Mmmm..." he moaned as he stuck his tongue inside her and slurped...

"Bazil... I'm cumming..." she moaned as he started sucking again... "Haa... Haa... Haa... Haa... Haaaaahhhh!"

"Uh uh..." Bazil said as he held her up by her ass to keep her from slumping down...

"Bazil..." she moaned as he continued licking and sucking softly...

"Answer me..." he breathed...

"You!" she moaned...

"Are you sure?"

"Yeesss...."

"Okay then..." he said as he stood up, kissed her, and put his tongue in her mouth...

"Mmmm..." she moaned...

"Come with me..." he said as he took her by the hand and led her into the living room. Bazil removed his slippers, took off his robe, dropped it on the floor, took off his pajamas, and stood in front of her naked. Beautiee walked over to him, pushed him down onto the couch, put the pillows on the floor, kneeled on the pillows, and took him in her mouth slowly...

"Got Damn..." he breathed as she took him all the way in her mouth and swirled her tongue around his shaft before she took him all the way out... "Yes Beautiee... Suck it..." he moaned as he put his hands in her hair and pushed her head back down on his dick... "Fuck... Beautiee..."

"Mmmm... Hmmm..." she moaned on his dick, pushing him over the edge...

"Uuuuggghhhh!" Beautiee continued sucking softly for a few moments until he called her name again... "Beautiee..."

"Yesss... Bazil..." she answered as she looked up at him...

"Come here..." he breathed as he pulled her up into a kiss... "What would you like to do next?"

"I want to go to News 12 and let them know this is over..."

"Really?"

"Yea..."

"Okay..."

"I still can't believe it..."

"Neither can I..."

"If anybody told me what I was in for when I married you..." Beautiee laughed...

"What's that supposed to mean?"

"I never expected to see your dead parents fuckin' in our backyard – let alone meet them..." she laughed... "It's a true romance with a happy ending..." she sighed...

"A true romance? A happy ending? I think you've had a little more than coffee..." Bazil laughed...

"Your parents came to ask for your help because they couldn't rest..."

"True..."

"All they wanted was to spend eternity together... but Clayton stood in their way..."

"True..."

"Don't you see? We saved their lives – in death – Oh my God!" she squealed as she jumped

81

up, ran into the library and turned on her computer...

"Beautiee – what are you doing?"

"I need to write these ideas before I forget them – and I need you to send me pictures of your parents on their wedding day so I can get them over to my cover designer – you know what – never mind – I'll just scan these pictures to my computer and send them over..." she said as she stood up and Bazil pulled her into a kiss...

"Mmmm... what was that for?" she breathed...

"I love you so much..."

"I love you to – but I need to do this..." she said as she went over to the wall and took down the pictures of his parents...

"Please Beautiee – be careful with those..."

"I will..." she said as she took her time taking them out the frame. Bazil watched as she scanned them to her computer and waited for her to finish... "Here..." she said as she handed him back the pictures and he put them in the frame and hung them back up... "When were your parents married?" she asked as she started typing...

"Sunday, March 23, 1930..."

"Okay – thanks..."

"Beautiee..."

"Yes Bazil..." she answered without stopping...

"We need to get ready...

"You get started – I'll join you in a few minutes..."

"You promise?"

"Yes – I promise – I need to get back to this!" she exclaimed...

"Okay, okay!" Bazil laughed as he headed upstairs...

"You ready for this?" Beautiee asked as they started walking across the parking lot at the train station in Norwalk...

"I'm ready if you are..."

"Okay – let's do this..." she said as she took his hand, they crossed the street, and ran right into Della Crews from News 12 Connecticut...

"Bazil! How are you?"

"I'm fine..."

"What brings you here?"

"Hello Della..." Beautiee said deliberately...

"Hello Mrs. Osgood – how are you?"

"I'm fine..." she sighed as Bazil pulled her close to him and put his arm around her...

"I was just going to have lunch – care to join me?"

"Another time..." Bazil said...

"I'm going to hold you to that..."

"Let us know when..." Beautiee said as she walked off...

"Let's go inside..." Bazil said as he took Beautiee by the hand, they walked up Cross Street, and went inside...

"Mr. Osgood – Mrs. Osgood – I thought you forgot about me..." Gwen laughed...

"We ran into Della..." Bazil laughed...

"Really? She told me she was going to lunch..."

"She invited us to join her..." Beautiee laughed...

"That woman will stop at nothing..." Gwen laughed, shaking her head...

"Let's go into your office before she gets back..." Bazil said...

"You're right – come with me..." she said as we followed her into her office...

"Hi Marissa – where's Gwen?" Della asked...

"I thought you were going to lunch?"

"I was..." she sighed...

"What happened?"

"They pissed me off – now I have an attitude – I'm hungry – and that's a bad combination!"

"I work with you – I know..." Marissa laughed...

"I'm sorry..."

"I have something that might make you feel better..."

"Do tell?" Della said as she slid over in the chair towards Marissa...

"The Osgood's are here..." she whispered...

"I knew it!" she snapped...

"I'm Gwen Edwards, News 12 Connecticut, bringing you an exclusive. I'm sitting here with Mr. & Mrs. Osgood – thank you both for coming in today..."

"Thank you for having us..."

"Mr. & Mrs. Osgood – it's always a pleasure – but I know our viewers are as curious as I am – what brings you here today?"

"As you know, we own Osgood Publishing..." Bazil answered...

"Yes – I'm aware..."

"After residents started reporting zombies in their backyard, we went to our office and checked the area surrounding our building..."

"Oh no – I hope everything was alright..."

"Unfortunately –it wasn't – we could see that zombies had been on the property..."

"What did you do?"

"The first thing we did was reduce the work hours for our staff. After we did that, we spoke with our landscapers and had them re-plant the flowers and bushes..."

"You weren't afraid they'd come back?"

"No..."

"Have you seen anything since?"

"Yesterday, we went to take a look and my landscapers told me everything was good..."

"How can you be sure they won't be back?"

"Because the supervisor told me he sprayed the area with Weed Killer sold by the Landscaping Corporation..."

"Mr. Osgood – are you telling me Weed Killer keeps the zombies from re-appearing?"

"According to our landscapers... yes..."

"Oh my God – is the Landscaping Corporation aware of this?"

"They will be after you air this interview..." Bazil laughed...

"Oh wow – okay – I'll get right on that..."

"There's something else we need to tell you..." Beautiee said...

"Yes Mrs. Osgood – go ahead..."

"Last night – we were in our backyard in the shed and..." Bazil took Beautiee's hand and squeezed it...

"Are you okay to continue?" Gwen asked as she touched her shoulder...

"Yes..." she breathed...

"Go ahead..."

"We came face to face with a zombie..."

"Oh my God! What did you do?"

"The only thing I could think of was to grab the Weed Killer and spray..."

"Did it kill the zombie?"

"It didn't kill the zombie – it burned it..."

"It burned it?"

"It started screaming and rubbing its eyes... and..."

"I picked up the spade and cracked its scull..." Bazil interrupted...

"Wait – the two of you actually killed a zombie?"

"Yes..." Bazil answered...

"Thank God I remembered what the supervisor told us about the Weed Killer..." Beautiee said...

"Thank God is right – I'm Gwen Edwards, News 12 Connecticut. As you just heard, Weed Killer, sold by the Landscaping Corporation, burns zombies and stops them from coming back when sprayed on lawns. News 12 Connecticut will continue to bring you updates..."

"Charles! Charles! Get in here!"

"I saw it..." Charles sighed...

"Isn't that great?" Theresa exclaimed...

"Yes - it is – I accused him of lying to our son and he actually did what he said he was going to do – that's just fucking great!"

CHAPTER 11

"Good morning..." Sam greeted as they walked in...

"Good morning Sam – staff meeting at 10..."

"Okay..." Sam said as he went down the hall to tell everyone else...

"Let's have breakfast in the cafeteria..." Beautiee said...

"Hmmm – you want breakfast today?"

"Yea..."

"Good morning Mr. & Mrs...." Jack said...

"Good morning..." they said in unison as Beautiee walked over to the counter and looked at the menu...

"Mrs. Osgood – you want breakfast? What's the occasion?"

"Ummm... I'm hungry..." she laughed...

"What can I get you?"

"I'd like a fried egg with Swiss melted on top, turkey bacon, turkey sausage, home fries, and a pancake..."

"Ummm..."

"I'll have what she's having..." Bazil laughed as he came up behind her, held her, and whispered in her ear... "You keep eating like that people might think you're pregnant..."

"Good morning Mrs. Osgood, good morning Mr. Osgood..." Joselyn said as she came in...

"Good morning..." Beautiee sighed...

"Good morning Joselyn..." Bazil said...

"Oh my goodness – are you having breakfast?"

"Yes Joselyn..."

"I'm getting coffee – would you like some?"

"Joselyn?"

"Yes Mrs. Osgood?"

"I'd love some coffee – and I need you to have a seat at the table with us..."

"Okay..." she sighed as she went to get them coffee and then she sat down at the table...

"Breakfast is ready..." Jack said...

"Thanks Jack – I got it..." Bazil said as he picked up the plates and brought them to the table and they sat down...

"Oh my goodness – you were hungry!" Joselyn said...

"Thank you for the coffee – I know you need to get ready for the staff meeting so I'll be quick..."

"Staff meeting?"

"Yes – at ten o'clock..."

"Sam didn't tell me!"

"It's okay – but I have something to tell you..."

"Okay – what project do you need me for this time?"

"I'm writing a book about Bazil's parents..."

"Oh wow – that's nice – I can't wait to read it!"

"It's going to focus on them showing up in our backward..."

"Ooohhh... okay..."

"I'll see you in the conference room..." Beautiee said as she started eating..."

"Oh – do you need me to leave?" Joselyn laughed...

"You can stay if you want – I just didn't want to be rude..." Beautiee laughed...

"I'll see you later..." Joselyn laughed as she left...

"How's your food?" Bazil asked...

"Delicious..." Beautiee answered as she continued eating...

"Better than mine?"

"No – but it's good..."

"It's just about 10..."

"Stop rushing me!" she laughed...

"How y'all doin'?" Jack asked...

"We're okay Jack..." Bazil answered...

"How's the food Mrs. Osgood?"

"Mmm hmmm..."

"Glad to hear that..." Jack laughed...

"Okay – I'm done..." Beautiee said as she rubbed her stomach...

"Good – c'mon – let's go..."

"Will you stop rushing me?" Beautiee laughed as she got up. Bazil pulled her to him and whispered in her ear...

"Never..."

"That tickles..." she laughed as they left the cafeteria and headed to the conference room. When they walked in, everyone got really quiet as they headed up to the front of the table..."

"Good morning..." Bazil said...

"Good morning..." they all said in unison...

"As you know, zombies have been showing up where and when we least expect them..."

"Uh huh..."

"Exactly..."

"Right..."

"If you've been watching News 12, you basically know what's been happening up to this point – but we called this meeting to give you the latest update..."

"Ooohhh..."

"Oh my God!"

"Shhh!"

"It's over..." Bazil said...

"It's over? Woo hoo!"

"Thank God!"

"Yeesss!"

"For the remainder of the month, we're going to continue with the hours we have in place – 9 a.m. to 3 p.m. – or 9 a.m. to 2 p.m. without lunch. Everyone will continue to get paid their normal salary and your benefits will not change – are there any questions?"

"I have a question..."

"Yes Shadajah?"

"How do you know it's over?"

"Earlier this week when we met with the staff, Sam and I walked around the building and we could tell that zombies had been in the parking lot. We spoke with the landscapers, the area has been treated with Weed Killer, and the zombies haven't returned..."

"Okay – I have another question..."

"Go ahead Shadajah..."

"Do you still have zombies in your backyard?"

"No – they're gone – which brings me to my next topic – if anyone calls with questions regarding zombies – please refer them to Joselyn – Joselyn will take a message and we'll take it from there...."

"Why would anybody call here about zombies?" A'Licia asked...

"Because it started with my parents..." Bazil answered...

"Oh yea – I forgot about that..."

"Before we end the meeting – I need everyone to follow this directive. We have a supply of Weed Killer in our supply room where the copier paper is kept – every employee is required to take one and use it in your back yard, your front yard, your parking lot, or anywhere else you see grass. Joselyn and Shadajah will coordinate the distribution of Weed Killer – everyone is required to sign for it and these forms will be kept on file. We should have enough for everyone but if we need more – we'll get it – are there any other questions? Okay – we're leaving for the day – if you need us, let Sam know and he'll get us – have a good day..." Bazil said as he took me by the hand and pulled me out the conference room...

"Bazil... wait..." Beautiee laughed...

"What's wrong?"

"Nothing – I just want to check something in the office..." she said as she hurried down to the office with Bazil right behind me... "Bazil – stop..." Beautiee laughed as he pushed her back against the door and locked it...

"No..." he breathed in her ear and then he stared kissing her on her neck...

"Bazil – stop..."

"Do you really want me to stop?"

"Yes..."

"Okay..." he sighed as he unlocked the door and went to sit down at his desk...

"I heard back from my cover designer – he sent a draft for me to look at..." she said as she hurried to her desk... "Oh my God..." I whispered...

"Can I see it?"

"Come take a look..." Bazil looked at the cover and started crying...

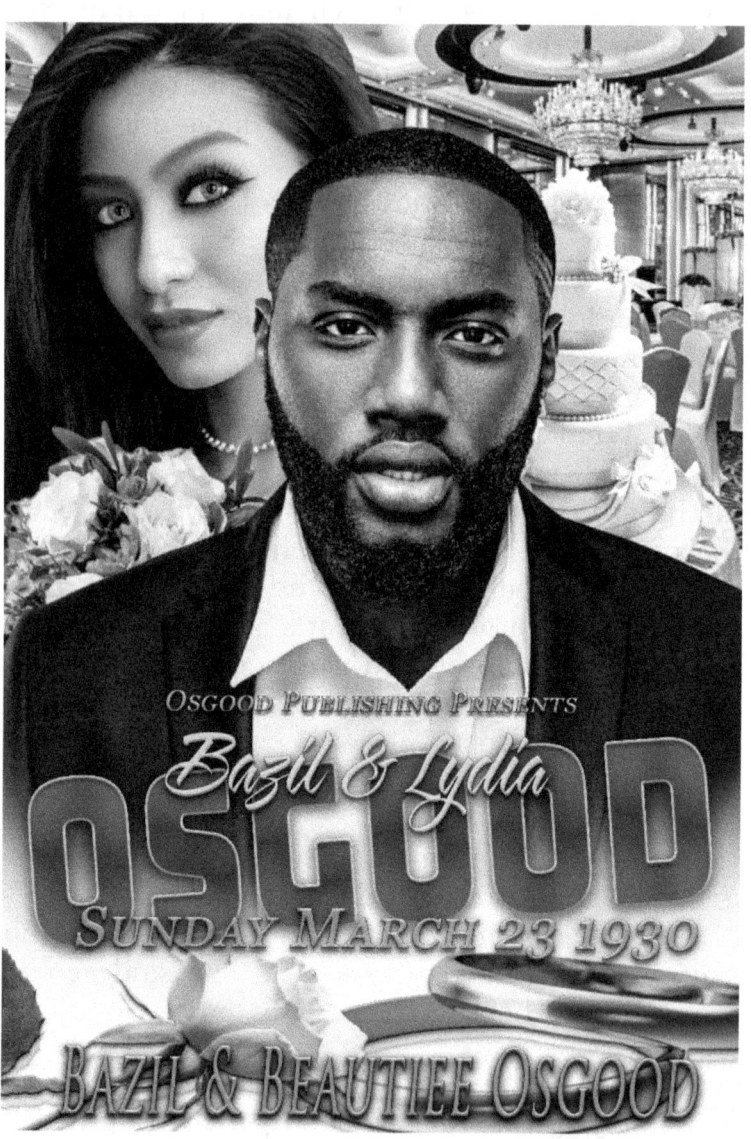

"You don't like it?"

"I love you so much!" he cried as he pulled her into a kiss and kissed her hard...

"I love you too..."

"I love it..."

"He's really good..."

"I want to offer him a contract – from now on – he does the covers for all our authors..."

"Oh wow – I can't wait to tell him!"

"Thank you for calling Osgood Publishing – this is Bazil..."

"Mutha Fuckaaaaa!" I heard as Bazil put the phone on speaker...

"Hello Liam..." Bazil laughed...

"Look man – I called to thank you..."

"That isn't necessary..."

"Yo – after what you said on News 12 – we rich! Sales are up! Stocks are up!"

"It was your product that started it..." Bazil laughed...

"I never thought I'd create a product that would be used to help men deal with impotence..." he laughed...

"Liam – the man that grows grass and raises dicks!" Bazil laughed...

"There you go with them jokes..." Liam laughed... "But seriously – I wanna tell you something..."

"What's that?"

"I just want you to know — when you're ready to publish your book — I'll give you permission to use my logo, my products, etc...."

"Of course you will — for a price..."

"You know me so well..."

"What do you want Liam?"

"I want a percentage..."

"You'll get a percentage of every book sold..."

"I'll be waiting for an agreement..."

"Thank you for calling Liam...."

"How much money does he want?" Beautiee asked...

"What he wants and what he's actually getting is two different things..." he answered as his phone rang again... "Hello Smalls..."

"Hello Bazil — I took care of the shares like you asked — and... um... Mutha Fuckaaaa!"

"You're welcome..." Bazil laughed...

"Have you heard from Liam yet?"

"He called me a Mutha Fucka earlier!" Bazil laughed...

"You know he wants a piece of Osgood Publishing — right?"

"What he wants and what he'll actually get are two different things..."

"Oh so you already knew what he was up to..."

"I'll send you over an agreement when we're ready to print..."

"Okay Bazil – we'll talk soon..."

"Mrs. Osgood?"

"Yes Mr. Osgood?"

"Let's go before this phone rings again..." he laughed...

CHAPTER 12

"I'm Scott McGee, Anchor and Managing Editor, News 12 Westchester. We interrupt our regularly scheduled programming to bring you the latest update. We now go live to Lisa LaRocca – go ahead Lisa..."

"Good morning Scott – I'm standing here at Rockefeller State Park Preserve in Pleasantville, New York. Employees were told to go home and have been advised to stay home until this can be explained..."

"Lisa – are they dead?"

"They're dead Scott..."

"Lisa – I can't believe what I'm seeing..."

"Scott – if I weren't standing here I wouldn't believe it either..."

"It looks like a scene from the Walking Dead..."

"It certainly does..."

"Thank you Lisa. I'm Scott McGee, News 12 Westchester. At this time, residents are being

98

warned and urged to continue to stay away from parks and graveyards. News 12 Westchester will continue to bring you updates. We now return to our regularly scheduled programming already in progress...”

"Momy!   Daddy!   Grandma!   Grandpa! Uncle   Bazil!   Auntie   Beautiee!”   the   kids squealed...

"Hello everybody!” Beautiee said...

"Hello everybody...” Bazil said...

"Hello Bazil...” Wayne said...

"Hello Wayne – I didn’t see you over there – hello Mary...”

"Hello Bazil, Beautiee...” Mary said...

"Hello Mary – oh my goodness – is that Sky?” I asked as I ran over to her and picked her up...

"Hi...” she said...

"Hello Sky...” Bazil said...

"Hi Starr Daddy...” Sky said...

"Come here Sky...” Wayne said...

"Yes Daddy?” Sky asked as she went over to him...

"This is Bazil... and this is Beautiee...”

"Bazil Starr Daddy?” she asked...

"Yes Sky...”

"Beautiee Starr Mommy?”

"No Sky – I’m Starr’s Mommy...” Mary said...

"Sky?”

"Yes Starr?”

"Beautiee is Jay, Joseph, and Joy's Mommy..."

"Ooohhh...." Sky said as she held her face in her hands and shook her head back and forth...

"Go play Sky..." Mary laughed...

"Okay Mommy – bye!" she said as she ran off to go play...

"We've been watching the news..." Wayne said...

"Hey everybody..." Charles said as he came in...

"Hey..." they all said in unison...

"Hi everybody..." Theresa said as she came in...

"Hi!" they all said in unison again...

"Is Chandler here yet?" Charles asked...

"Not yet..." Starr answered...

"Hi Daddy!" Lil Charles said...

"Hi Lil' Charles..."

"Are we leaving?"

"Not yet..." Theresa answered...

"Okay – bye!" he said and then he ran off to go play...

"Are they always like this?" Mary laughed...

"Always..." Theresa laughed...

"Hey y'all!" Keisha said as she came in...

"Hi everybody – bye!" Amina said as she ran off to play... "Hey y'all!" Troy said as he came in...

"Hey..." they all said in unison...

"Chandler!" Starr exclaimed as she ran to the door, threw her arms around Chandler, and kissed him...

"Hello to you too..." he said as he kissed her... "Hey everybody..." Chandler said...

"Hey Chandler!" they all said in unison..."

"Daddy!   Uncle Chandler!" the kids squealed when they saw him....

"Hi, hi..." he said as they all ran back to play...

"We saw you on News 12..." Chandler said...

"You watch News 12 at work?" Charles asked...

"We keep it on all day..."

"I didn't see it yet..." Starr said...

"Le'me put it on for y'all..." Chandler said as he turned on the television and turned to News 12...

"I'm Gwen Edwards, News 12 Connecticut, bringing you an exclusive. I'm sitting here with Mr. & Mrs. Osgood – thank you both for coming in today..."

"Thank you for having us..."

"Mr. & Mrs. Osgood – it's always a pleasure – but I know our viewers are as curious as I am – what brings you here today?"

"As you know, we own Osgood Publishing..."

"Yes – I'm aware..."

"After residents started reporting zombies in their backyard, we went to our office and checked the area surrounding our building..."

"Oh no – I hope everything was alright..."

"Unfortunately –it wasn't – we could see that zombies had been on the property..."

"What did you do?"

"The first thing we did was reduce the work hours for our staff. After we did that, we spoke with our landscapers and had them re-plant the flowers and bushes..."

"You weren't afraid they'd come back?"

"No..."

"Have you seen anything since?"

"Yesterday, we went to take a look and my landscapers told me everything was good..."

"How can you be sure they won't be back?"

"Because the supervisor told me he sprayed the area with Weed Killer sold by the Landscaping Corporation..."

"Mr. Osgood – are you telling me Weed Killer keeps the zombies from re-appearing?"

"According to our landscapers... yes..."

"Oh my God – is the Landscaping Corporation aware of this?"

"They will be after you air this interview..." Bazil laughed...

"Oh wow – okay – I'll get right on that..."

"There's something else we need to tell you..." Beautiee said...

"Yes Mrs. Osgood – go ahead..."

"Last night – we were in our backyard in the shed and..."

"Are you okay to continue?"

"Yes..." I breathed...

"Go ahead..."

"We came face to face with a zombie..."

"Oh my God! What did you do?"

"The only thing I could think of was to grab the Weed Killer and spray..."

"Did it kill the zombie?"

"It didn't kill the zombie – it burned it..."

"It burned it?"

"It started screaming and rubbing its eyes... and..."

"I picked up the spade and cracked its scull..." Bazil interrupted..."

"Wait – the two of you actually killed a zombie?"

"Yes..." Bazil answered...

"Thank God I remembered what the supervisor told us about the Weed Killer..." Beautiee said...

"Thank God is right – I'm Gwen Edwards, News 12 Connecticut. As you just heard, Weed Killer, sold by the Landscaping Corporation, burns zombies and stops them from coming back when sprayed on lawns. News 12 Connecticut will continue to bring you updates..."

"I guess Lil' Charles can go back to school now..." Charles said...

"They can all go back to school..." Keisha said...

"Are they all in the same class?" Wayne asked...

"They're split between two classes across from each other..." Bazil answered...

"What if they give you a hard time?" Mary asked...

"I'm not worried..." Bazil said... "Grandchildren front and center!" Bazil boomed. Mary and Wayne watched as Chelsea, Kalliyah, and Chandler Jr. ran into the living room, lined up, and saluted... "One... two... three..."

"HUGS!" they squealed as they ran to hug them and then they started to run back to play but Bazil stopped them...

"Ummm - where's everybody going?"

"We goin' back inside Grandpa..." Chandler Jr. said...

"You can go back inside after you hug your grandparents..."

"We hug you already..."

"Yes you did – but you didn't hug Grandma Mary and Grandpa Wayne..."

"Ohhh..." Chandler Jr. said as they ran over to hug them... "Sorry Grandma, sorry Grandpa..."

"That's okay..." Wayne said...

"Starr Daddy Bazil my Grandpa?" Sky asked...

"No Sky..." Wayne answered...

"I don't have Grandpa?" she asked with tears in her eyes..."

"Come here Sky..." Beautiee said as she picked her up... "You have grandparents – but they're not here..."

"They home?"

"Why don't you go inside and play - the kids are going home soon..." Beautiee said...

"Okay..." she said as Beautiee put her down and she skipped off...

"That was close!" Mary laughed...

"Mommy!" Jay exclaimed as he came into the living room...

"Yes Jay?"

"We can go home?" he asked excitedly...

"Yes Jay..." Bazil answered...

"You don't have to go back to work?"

"Not tonight..."

"Yeeaaa!" he squealed and then he ran down the hall...

"How long have they been here?" Wayne asked...

"Two weeks..."

"I don't think I could stand it..." Wayne said...

"We did what we had to do..." Bazil said...

"When Starr told me you had zombies in your backyard I didn't believe it..." Mary said...

"We had one downstairs..." Chandler said...

"Oh my God! Here?" Mary asked...

"Yes..."

"What the hell was it doing here?"

105

"Who knows?"

"Thank God it's over!" Theresa exclaimed...

"Okay Zombie Killa!" Troy laughed...

"Oh shit – I like that – Zombie Killa!" Keisha laughed...

"It was actually the Weed Killer..." Bazil said...

"I'm still in shock – how can you be so calm?" Wayne asked...

"The only answer I have for that is my wife – I couldn't've done it without her..."

"I think you can do anything you put your mind to..." Beautiee said...

"You're right – I can do anything I put my mind to – but if I didn't have you to keep me sane..."

"I'd feel sorry for them zombies!" Charles laughed...

"Zombie Killa! Starring Bazil Osgood!" Troy laughed...

"Oh shit – I can see your costume now!" Charles laughed...

"Zombie Killa to the rescue!" Chandler laughed...

"I guess I've been called worse..." Bazil laughed....

"I know we're laughing – but it is an idea..." Wayne said...

"It is..." Bazil agreed...

"Have you ever done any acting?" Wayne asked...

"I have..."

"Yea... I could see it..."

"What are we eating – I'm hungry..." Starr said...

"We could go out if you want..." Chandler said...

"I don't really wanna go out..." Beautiee sighed...

"You don't?" Bazil asked...

"No – I just wanna go home..."

"You alright Beautiee?" Keisha asked...

"Yea..."

"Okay then – we'll go home – Jay – Joseph – Joy – we're leaving..." Bazil called as he stood up...

"Noooo...." Chelsea cried as she came running into the living room...

"Chelsea?" What's wrong?" Chandler asked as he pulled her into a hug...

"I don't want them to go home!"

"Awww – you can come with them if it's okay with Mom and Dad..." Bazil said...

"Can we Daddy? Please?"

"Starr..." Chandler started to ask...

"Okay – bye!" she laughed. Chelsea went running down the hall...

"Guess what – Mommy and Daddy said we can go to Grandpa's house!"

"Yeaaa!"

"Mommy?" Sky asked as she came into the living room...

"Yes Sky?"

"I go with family?"

107

"Well... umm...." Mary stuttered...

"If you want to come, that's fine..." Beautiee said. Keisha looked at her like a deer caught in headlights...

"Can I go Daddy?" Lil' Charles asked...

"Yes Charles – you can go too..."

"Okay – how we doin' this – your car cain't big enough for all o'them!" Chandler laughed...

"You're right – that's why you're coming with your children..." Bazil said as they all bust out laughing...

"I'm Della Crews, Anchor for News 12 Connecticut. We interrupt our regularly scheduled programming to bring you the latest update. We now go live to Roxanne Evans – go ahead Roxanne..."

"Good afternoon Della – I'm here at Milford Green where – hold on a minute – I'll let you see for yourself..."

"Oh my God – are those dead zombies?"

"That's exactly what they are Della..."

"Do you have any idea how long they've been there?"

"From what I've been told – the Green was fine yesterday during the Arts and Crafts Festival. The Milford Concert Band had an event, residents came from all over, and everyone had a great time..."

"Roxanne – I'm in shock – I can't imagine going from the Arts and Crafts Festival to dead zomies..."

"Della – I'm leaving now – just in case..."

"I'm Della Crews, News 12 Connecticut. At this time, residents are urged to continue to stay away from parks and graveyards. News 12 Connecticut will continue to bring you updates. We now return to our regularly scheduled programming already in progress..."

CHAPTER 13

"We're home!" Jay squealed as soon as we opened the door... "I wanna go to my room!"

"Me too!" Joseph said...

"I wanna go to my room!" Joy said as they started running upstairs...

"Me too!" Lil' Charles said followed by Chandler Jr. and Amina...

"C'mon Sky..." Chelsea said as she took Sky's left hand, Kalliyah took her right hand, and they went upstairs...

"I'm surprised she wanted to come..." Mary laughed...

"She knows she's with family..." Keisha said...

"We facetime so she knows who everyone is..." Starr said...

"This is nice..." Wayne said...

"Thank you..." Bazil said...

"Keisha – I need your help with something in the library – Starr – could you take your mother in the living room?" Beautiee asked...

"Sure – c'mon..." Starr said as Mary and Theresa followed her...

"Where you want us at?" Chandler asked...

"Wherever your father tells you to go – c'mon Keisha..." Beautiee said as she pulled Keisha into the library and closed the door...

"C'mon – I'll get us some Henney..." Bazil laughed...

"Okay!" Charles laughed...

"Wow – this is really nice..." Wayne said...

"Thank you..." Bazil said... "Ladies – there's some Moscato in the kitchen..."

"Thank you Daddy!" Starr said as she got up and went into the kitchen followed by Mary and Theresa...

"Aiight – what's goin' on?" Keisha asked...

"I'm pregnant..."

"Okay – I get it..."

"You get what?"

"I was wondering what the hell was wrong with you..." she laughed...

"Oh because I said Sky could come?"

"Hell yea!"

"She wants to be with the kids – what was I supposed to do?"

"Be careful Beautiee – you know how you get when you're pregnant..."

"What's that supposed to mean?"

111

"You and Bazil are on another honeymoon – but don't let those rose-colored glasses cloud your vision..."

"Keisha!"

"I'on wanna hurt your feelins – I just want you to remember who Mary is..."

"How could I forget? She's Starr's mother!" Beautiee laughed...

"She's also the woman that wants your husband..."

"You really think after everything that happened – even though she has a husband that loves her unconditionally – the child she always wanted to give him – that she still wants my husband?"

"You right – she has all that – and she loves her husband – but she want's yours..."

"I need a glass of wine..." Beautiee sighed...

"You don't need no wine – you need to eat..."

"I know..." she sighed again...

"Uh uh – stop that..." Keisha said as she pulled Beautiee into a hug and rubbed her back...

"Beautiee? You okay?" Bazil asked...

"Did you miss me?" she asked as she opened the door...

"Always..." he answered as he kissed her...

"C'mon – you said something about wine..." Keisha said as she took Beaitiee's hand and pulled her away from Bazil...

"Hi Beautiee..." Starr laughed...

"Enjoying the wine?" Beautiee asked...

"It's good!" she slurred...

"Beautiee – I love your kitchen – do those French doors lead to the backyard?" Mary asked...

"Yes Mommy..." Starr answered...

"Show me where the zombies were..." Mary said as she went to open the doors and Keisha stopped her...

"We ain't come over here for that – we came to eat and have wine..." she said as she put her arm around Mary and guided her back to the island...

"You're right – so what are we eating?"

"I could go for some seafood..." Beautiee said...

"Ohhh... that sounds good – what will the kids eat?"

"Same thing we eat!' Theresa laughed...

"What are we eating?" Charles asked...

"Whatever the ladies want..." Chandler answered...

"Why can't we have something different?" Wayne asked...

"You haven't been married that long – have you?" Troy asked...

"Ummm... no – but what does that have to do with..."

"Wayne – you go out to dinner with Mary – right?" Bazil asked...

"Yes we do..."

113

"And when you go out to dinner – what happens when you get the menu?"

"She orders one thing I order another thing, and... ooohhhh..." he answered as they all started laughed...

"Oh – le'me taste that!" Chandler said...

"Oh that's good – I should'a ordered that!" Charles said...

"Le'me get some more..." Troy said...

"Is it always like that?" Wayne asked...

"Only when they get together and start drinking wine..." Bazil answered as they all laughed...

"Honey – we want seafood..." Beautiee said as we walked into the living room...

"We can have seafood..." Bazil said...

"I don't know if Sky will eat seafood...." Wayne said...

"That's what you said about pancakes!" Bazil laughed...

"You're right..." Wayne laughed...

"I'll call Captain's Catch..." Bazil said as he picked up his cell phone... "Yes – this is Bazil... I'm fine... Me too.... I'm hungry... Yes I know what we want... Okay – I'll hold... Yes I'm ready... Eight orders of hotdogs and fries... yes that's right... two orders of fish bites, two orders of bay scallops, two orders of clam strips, two orders of butterfly shrimp, two calamari platters, two cod platters, two sole platters, and a tray of fish tacos... Okay I'll hold... Yes – that's right... Yes – same card... Okay – thanks..."

"Damn..." Beautiee sighed...

"It does sound good..." Starr said...

"It is!" Keisha exclaimed...

"I can't wait..." Theresa said...

"Thanks for getting hotdogs Bazil – Sky is so finicky..." Mary said...

"She wouldn't be so finicky if she was around more..." Beautiee said...

"What's that supposed to mean?"

"I didn't mean to offend you – It's just that the kids eat just about everything we eat because they get curious, they taste it, and then they like it..."

"We're going to try that..." Wayne said...

"I don't know Wayne – you know how she is..."

"We'll let her try it – if she doesn't like it – she doesn't have to eat it..."

"Okay..." Mary laughed... "We'll see..."

"I know I'm gonna eat it..." Chandler said as he looked at Starr mischievously...

"Chandler!" Starr exclaimed...

"What? What'd I say?" he asked as we all laughed...

"Girl stop bein' all shy like you still a virgin!" Keisha laughed...

"Thank God Bazil wasn't hungry they day we got caught!" Beautiee laughed...

"Oh shit!" Troy exclaimed as we all bust out laughing...

"Oh my God! I'm sorry!" Starr exclaimed...

"Starr – it's okay – I love you – but for real though..." Beautiee said and then they started laughing again...

"That's it – I'm putting a bolt lock on that mutha fucka - Lil' Charles ain't never gonna catch me eatin!" Charles laughed...

"We've been locking our door since Christmas..." Wayne said...

"Christmas?" Bazil asked...

"Remember when you said Jay was walking around the house saying fuck, fuck fuck?"

"Oh yea!" Bazil exclaimed as we all laughed...

"Mommy?" Jay asked as he came into the living room...

"Yes Jay?"

"I wanna eat – I'm hungry..." That was it...

"Aahhaaaaaa! Aahhaaaaa! Aahhaaaa! Aahhaaaaaa! Aahhaaaaa! Aahhaaaa!"

"What's so funny?"

"Nothing..." Bazil answered... "We ordered something – we're gonna eat soon..."

"Okay!" Jay squealed as he ran out and went back upstairs...

"Beautiee – I'd love to see the rest of the house – if that's alright..." Mary said. Keisha and Beautiee looked at each other before Beautiee spoke...

"I'm enjoying our wine time..."

116

"I've noticed you haven't had any wine..."

"I'm a light weight – if I drink before I eat – it goes right to my head..."

"Mommy!" Sky called...

"I'm coming Sky..." Mary said as she jumped up to run upstairs...

"C'mon ladies!" Beautiee said as they all went upstairs behind Mary...

"Sky? Where are you?" Mary called out...

"I'm in the bathroom..."

"Are you okay?" Mary asked as she went down the hall and knocked on the door...

"I need to wash my hands..."

"I'm coming in..." Mary said and then she went into the bathroom...

"Might as well give you the tour – not much to it though..." Beautiee said as they waited for Mary and Sky...

"Shit – this is nice!" Theresa said...

"Thank you Theresa..."

"She's okay – she couldn't reach the sink..." Mary said as she came out and Sky ran back to play...

"Okay so this is the bathroom..." Beautiee laughed as we all squeezed inside... "If you'll follow me down the hall this is the laundry room..."

"You have laundry upstairs? Oh that's nice!" Theresa said...

"Sure is – we wash, dry, and put away..." Keisha laughed...

"You have laundry upstairs too?" Theresa asked...

"All the houses on this block have laundry upstairs..." Keisha answered...

"Over here is Joy's room..." Beautiee said as they went into the room...

"Hi!" the girls said in unison..."

"Hello..." they all answered...

"And this is the boys' room..." Beautiee said as they went into the room...

"Hi!" the boys said in unison...

"Hello..." they all answered...

"Where's your room?" Mary asked...

"I'm not showing my room..."

"Why not?" Theresa asked... "You have a few unmentionables on the floor?"

"Girl – how'd you know?" Beautiee laughed, silently thanking God for the save...

"Ladies, kids – the food's here!" Bazil yelled upstairs...

"Coming!" the kids yelled as they all ran past us and ran downstairs...

"I guess they're hungry..." Mary laughed as we all headed downstairs...

"Kids at the table!" Bazil boomed...

"Yes Grandpa!"

"Yes Daddy!"

"Yes Uncle Bazil!"

"Yes Bazil Starr Daddy!"

"Okay – here you go..." Chandler said as he put some of the hotdogs and French fries on the table and Wayne put the rest...

"Thank you!" they all said in unison...

"I'm thirsty..." Sky said...

"Juice after you eat..." Keisha said...

"Ladies – help yourselves..." Bazil said...

"Bazil – come with me..." Beautiee said as she took his hand and pulled him out the kitchen and into the foyer...

"Beautiee – what's wrong?"

"Did you ever fuck Mary in this house?"

"Yes..." he sighed...

"Does Wayne know?"

"No..."

"Thank you..."

"For what?"

"The truth..."

"Can we eat now?"

"Yes – we can eat now..." she answered as she took him by the hand and pulled him back into the kitchen...

"Here Beautiee, here Daddy – I didn't know what you wanted so I gave you some of everything..." Starr said as she handed us plates...

"Thank you – I'm starving!" Beautiee exclaimed as she started eating...

"There you are! Charles exclaimed... "You got any more Henney?"

"I'll show you where it is..." Bazil laughed as he went into the living room with his plate and Charles followed...

"C'mon Starr..." Beautiee said as she headed into the living room and Starr followed...

"You good Beautiee?" Keisha asked...

"I'm good..." she sighed...

"I know I'm good – that food was delicious!" Theresa said...

"Damn sure was..." Troy said...

"I wish they had a Captain's Catch in Canada..." Wayne said...

"Mommy?"

"Yes Chelsea..." Starr answered...

"Can we spend the night?"

"That's up to your grandparents..."

"Grandpa? Can we spend the night? Please?"

"Sure..." Bazil said...

"Grandpa said we can spend the night!" Chelsea squealed...

"Yeaaah!" all the kids squealed...

"Mommy? I stay with family?" Sky asked...

"Are you sure Sky?" Wayne asked... "If you start crying we can't come get you because it's far...

"I stay with family..." she answered and then she ran back upstairs...

"We're gonna have to get a bigger place..." Wayne said...

"We are?" Mary asked...

"We don't have a choice – once they all come to visit – Sky won't want anybody to leave..." Wayne laughed.

CHAPTER 14

"I'm Scott McGee, Anchor and Managing Editor, News 12 Westchester. We interrupt your regularly scheduled programming to bring you this update. At this time, News 12 is happy to report that in the last 24 hours, there haven't been any reports or sitings of zombies. DPW is currently working with Parks and Recreation to remove dead zombies from all parks, graveyards, and homes of residents in Westchester County. At this time, News 12 is asking all residents to call DPW if you have a dead zombie on your property to schedule a pick up. At the request of DPW, News 12 is asking all residents – please – DO NOT put dead zombies in garbage bags or cans – DPW is working round the clock to schedule pick-ups and remove dead zombies as quickly as possible. At the request of Parks and Recreation, News 12 is requesting that all residents continue to stay away from all parks and graveyards. Parks and graveyards are currently being sprayed with Weed Killer from the Landscaping Corporation and we are continuing to see progress. Parks and Recretation has advised News 12 that they expect parks will be open sometime next week. News 12 has also been advised that funerals, burials, and cremations will begin at all funeral homes throughout Westchester County starting Monday. I'm Scott McGee, News 12 Westchester. Thank you for watching. We now return to our regularly scheduled programming already in progress..."

"Bazil... Fuck..."

"Shhh..." he breathed as he continued stroking her slowly and deliberately...

"I can't help it..." Beautiee moaned. Bazil pulled her to him, covered her mouth with his, pushed his tongue in her mouth, and fucked her deeper... "MMMMMMMMM!" she moaned in his mouth as her body trembled and her legs shook...

"MMMMMMMPPPHHHH!" he moaned in her mouth as his body shook...

"You can't fuck me like that and expect me to be quiet..." she panted...

"I know..." he breathed as he kissed her...

"We really need to do something..."

"I know..." he breathed as he kissed her again...

"Bazil..."

"Yes... Beautiee..."

"Are you listening to me?"

"I took care of it..." he breathed as he kissed her again...

"You did?"

"They'll be here later today..."

"Mmmm.... who?"

"Home Depot..."

"What..." she started to say but Bazil interrupted her by kissing her...

"We're getting a solid wood door for the bedroom..."

"Mmmm hmmm..."

"They're going to install a sound-proof interior wall right behind our headboard..."

"Mmmm hmmm..."

"Once they do that..."

"Mmmm hmmm..."

"We can make as much noise as we want..."

"Grandma!" Chelsea called...

"Yes Chelsea?"

"Sky's crying..."

"I'm coming..." Beautiee sighed as they both got up and went down the hall to Joy's room...

"Good morning!" they all said in unison..."

"Good morning..." Bazil said...

"Good morning girls..." Beautiee said as they walked into the room... "Hey Sky..." Beautiee said as she picked her up...

"I want Mommy..." she cried...

"Mommy's sleeping..."

"Mommy's sleeping?"

"Yes..."

"Mommy come get me when she wake up?"

"Yes..."

"Okay... she said and then Beautiee put her down...

"Grandpa – can we have pancakes?" Chelsea asked...

"Sure..." Bazil said...

"Okay – we're going to check on the boys – we'll be right back..." Beautiee said as they went to check on them...

"Good morning!" they all said in unison...

"Good morning..." Bazil said...

"Good morning boys..." Beautiee said as they walked into the room... "Hi Mommy! Hi Daddy!" Jay beamed...

"Good morning – how'd you sleep?" Bazil asked...

"I didn't get scared! Wanna see?" Jay beamed as he ran over to the window, snatched the curtain open and showed them...

"That's good..." Beautiee said.

"I'm hungry..." Chandler Jr. said...

"We're going to have pancakes..." Bazil said...

"Yeeeaaah!" they squealed as they ran out the room and down the hall...

"Wash those hands!" Bazil boomed...

"Yeesss..." they all said in unison...

"C'mon Sky – we have to wash our hands..." Chelsea said as they got in line...

"Beautiee – I need to ask you something..." Bazil said as they went to the other end of the hall...

"Yes Bazil?"

"What was that about yesterday?"

"I'm sorry..."

"You have nothing to be sorry for..."

"When we got here yesterday... I took Keisha in the library and told her I was pregnant..."

"Aww..." Bazil said as he pulled her into a kiss...

"She told me don't be fooled by Mary because she still wants you..."

"Oh... I see..."

"Mary asked me to give her a tour of the house and I didn't really want to so I told her I was enjoying our wine time – but then Sky called her because she needed help in the bathroom so she ran upstairs – I couldn't stop her so I told everybody I might as well give them a tour..."

"Okay..."

"So when we got upstairs, I showed them the kids' rooms and the laundry room and then Mary asked to see our room... and I said I'm not showing my room..."

"Come here..." Bazil said as he pulled her into a hug and held her...

"So Theresa asked if I had unmentionables on the floor and I went with it..."

"I'm sorry..."

"She was in our bedroom – wasn't she?"

126

"Yes..."

"Wayne has no idea who he married..."

"If he ever finds out... he'll kill her..."

"He loves her with all his heart..."

"And I love you with all of mine..." Bazil breathed as he kissed her...

"Grandpa loves Grandma..." Chandler Jr. giggled...

"I sure do..." Bazil said...

"Grandma – Sky needs help..." Chelsea said...

"C'mon everybody –let's go into the kitchen..." Bazil said and then they followed him downstairs...

"I'm here Sky..." Beautiee said as she went into the bathroom...

"I can't reach..." she said...

"C'mon..." Beautiee said as she picked her up and held her so she could turn on the water and wash her hands...

"Thank you Mommy Beautiee..." she beamed...

"Aww... you're welcome..." Beautiee said as she took her hand and we went downstairs into the kitchen...

"Just in time!" Bazil beamed when we walked in...

"Yeaaah!" the kids squealed...

"Sky – sit at the table so you can eat..." Bazil said...

"Okay Daddy Bazil..." she said and then she went to sit at the table...

"Here you go..." Bazil said as he placed the pancakes in front of her...

"Mmmm..." she said as she took a bite...

"I made coffee..." Bazil said as he handed Beautiee a cup of coffee...

"Thank you Daddy..." Beautiee said as she smiled at him mischievously...

"I want coffee..." Amina said...

"Me too!" Joseph said...

"Kids don't drink coffee – right Daddy?" Jay asked...

"That's right..." Bazil answered...

"Can we have juice?" Chelsea asked...

"You can have juice when you finish your pancakes..." Bazil said...

"Beautiee – sit down so I can feed you..."

"Okay Daddy..."

"That's not your Daddy!" Jay laughed...

"I know Jay – Mommy's just being silly..." Beautiee said as they started eating...

"I finished!" Lil Charles exclaimed...

"You'll get juice as soon as we finish eating..." Bazil said...

"Okay..." Charles sighed...

"I'll get it..." Beautiee said...

"Beautiee – sit..." Bazil said as he touched her hand...

"Okay..." Beautiee sighed. Bazil finished his food, finished his coffee, and then he got up...

"Yeaaahhh!" the kids squealed...

"Juice for you... you...." he said as he placed the cups on the table... "You... you... you... you... you... and you..."

"Thank you!" they all said in unison as they drank their juice. When they were finished, Chelsea got up from the table and started to leave...

"Chelsea..."

"Yes Grandpa?"

"What do we do when we finish eating?"

"We clean up..." she sighed...

"That's right..." Bazil said. Chelsea opened the dishwasher, pulled out the top tray, put her cup in the tray, and then she put her plate and fork in the bottom tray... "Good girl..."

"Me too..." Sky said as she got up and tried to put her cup in the tray but she couldn't reach it...

"I'll help you..." Kalliyah said as she got up along with the rest of the children and they put their dishes in the dishwasher...

"Good job..." Bazil said...

"We have to get dressed?" Amina asked...

"No – you can go back upstairs and play..." Bazil answered...

"Yeaaa!" they squealed as they ran upstairs...

"Who is it?" Beautiee asked...

"It's Home Depot..."

"Bazil – Home Depot is here..." she said as she opened the door...

"Good morning Mrs. Osgood – I'm Roy Thompson – we're here to sound proof your bedroom?" he asked...

"Yes – come on in..."

"This is Jerry – he's going to assist me..." he said as Bazil came to the door...

"Good morning Mr. Osgood..." Roy said...

"Good morning Roy..."

"This is Jerry – my assistant..."

"Good morning, good morning..." Jerry said...

"Come with me – I'll show you where our room is..." Bazil said as they followed him upstairs and Beautiee went to get more coffee...

"My goodness – I see why you want us to sound proof your room..." Roy laughed... "How many children do you have?"

"Eight..." Bazil answered...

"God bless ya..." Roy said as they went to work..."

"Here..." Beautiee said as she handed Bazil a cup of coffee... "How's everything going?" she asked...

"We're just about done..." Roy answered...

"Really?"

"Yes – we've already insulated the wall – once we attach the panel – we're done – you just need to let it sit for 8 hours..."

"Oh wow..."

"Now all we need to do is change this door for that solid door, and then we're done..."

"Nice..." she said as she watched them install the door...

"Go ahead – try the door out..." Roy said...

"Oh my goodness – Bazil – try the door..." Beautiee said...

"Oh wow – that's heavy..."

"This is where you lock it – push here to lock, push here to unlock..." Roy said...

"What if we get locked out?" Beautiee asked...

"Jerry – gi'me a penny..." Roy said. Jerry gave him a penny and we watched Roy use the penny to turn the lock...

"Oh shit!" Bazil laughed...

"We make all the bedroom dors this way – especially when there are children in the home..."

"Children front and center!" Bazil boomed...

"Yes sir!" the children said in unison as they all lined up and saluted...

"Yes Daddy Bazil..." Sky said as she came out, got in line, and saluted...

"Would you look at that? They're adorable!" Roy exclaimed...

"I want you to go in the room, close the door, and yell as loud as you can..." Bazil said...

"Don't jump on that bed!" Beautiee yelled as they all ran in the room and slammed the door...

"Yeeaaah! Woo hooo! Aaaahhaaa! Aaaahaaa!"

"What'd you think?" Roy asked...

131

"You can barely hear them..." Bazil said...

"Now imagine you're sleeping in while they're down the hall — they can make all the noise they want — and so can you..." Roy said as he winked...

"Thank you Roy..." Bazil said...

"You're welcome..."

"Thank you Jerry..."

"You're welcome..."

"Let the wall set for eight hours — other than that if you have any problems, just give me a call..." Roy said as they went downstairs...

"Thank you again..." Bazil said as they left... "Children front and center!" he boomed...

"Yes sir!" they all squealed...

"Go to your rooms and play until your parents come..."

"Yeeaaa!" they all squealed as they ran down the hall...

"Mrs. Osgood?"

"Yes Mr. Osgood?"

"Come with me..." he said as he took her by the hand, pulled her into the room, and closed the door. Bazil pushed her back against the door, put his body against hers, kissed her, and whispered in her ear... "Eight hours from now..." He began kissing her on her neck and then he whispered in her ear again... "I'm going to bring you back in here..." He began kissing her on her neck again and then he whispered in her ear for the 3rd time... "And I'm going to make you scream..."

"I'm Della Crews, News 12 Connecticut. We interrupt your regularly scheduled programming to bring you this update. At this time, News 12 is happy to report that in the last 24 hours, there haven't been any reports or sitings of zombies. DPW is currently working with Parks and Recreation to remove dead zombies from all parks, graveyards, and homes of residents in Fairfield County. At this time, News 12 is asking all residents to call DPW if you have a dead zombie on your property to schedule a pick up. At the request of DPW, News 12 is asking all residents – please – DO NOT put dead zombies in garbage bags or cans – DPW is working round the clock to schedule pick-ups and remove dead zombies as quickly as possible. At the request of Parks and Recreation, News 12 is requesting that all residents continue to stay away from all parks and graveyards. Parks and graveyards are currently being sprayed with Weed Killer from the Landscaping Corporation and we are continuing to see progress. Parks and Recretation has advised News 12 that they expect parks will be open sometime next week. News 12 has also been advised that funerals, burials, and cremations will begin at all funeral homes throughout Fairfield County starting Monday. I'm Della Crews, News 12 Connecticut. Thank you for watching. We now return to our regularly scheduled programming already in progress..."

CHAPTER 15

"Osgood Publishing – this is Bazil..." he answered as he put the phone on speaker...

"Mr. Osgood – this is Tara Rosenbloom, News 12 Westchester..."

"Hello Ms. Rosenbloom – what can I do for you?"

"I'd like to interview you and your wife..."

"As much as I'd love to, I don't think we have anything else to say..."

"Let me worry about that..."

"Beautiee? What do you think?"

"Let's do it..."

"Okay Ms. Rosenbloom – we'll do it..." Bazil said...

"Great! How about this afternoon?"

"This afternoon? Okay – how's 3 p.m.?"

"That's fine - Mr. Osgood – I'd like to do a live interview in your office – would that be okay?"

"Sure..."

"Great! I'll see you at 3 p.m."

"See you then..." Bazil said as he hung up... "Oh boy..."

"We'll be fine..." Beautiee said...

"Mrs. Osgood?"

"Yes Joselyn?"

"News 12 is here..."

"Okay..." Beautiee said as she got up and opened the door... "Hi Tara – welcome to Osgood Publishing – come on in..."

"Hello Mrs. Osgood – it's great to meet you – thanks for agreeing to do the interview..."

"You're welcome – please call me Beautiee..."

"Thank you Beautiee..."

"Hello Ms. Rosenbloom..." Bazil said as he came into the office...

"Hello Mr. Osgood – it's great to meet you – please call me Tara..."

"Please call me Bazil..."

"Would you like something to drink? I can take you to the cafeteria while they set up..." Beautiee said...

"Sure – thank you..."

"Right this way..." Bazil said as he led the way...

"Ooohh... you're from News 12..." A'Licia said when she saw them...

"Hi – I'm Tara Rosenbloom..." Tara said as she extended her hand...

"Hi Tara – I'm A'Licia Henley..."

"Nice meeting you..." Tara said. They continued down the hall to the cafeteria and Tara looked around... "This is nice..."

"Thank you – help yourself to whatever you like..." Bazil said...

"Thank you – Beautiee – what would you suggest?"

"Coffee..." Beautiee answered as she got a cup...

"Coffee it is..." Tara said as she got a cup...

"I might as well join you..." Bazil said as he got a cup and then we headed back to the office...

"Okay – are you ready?" she asked...

"Ready..." they both answered in unison...

"Recording in five, four, three, two... good afternoon. I'm Tara Rosenbloom, News 12 Westchester. I'm sitting here with Bazil and Beautiee Osgood at Osgood Publishing – thank you for having me..."

"Thank you for being here..." Bazil said...

"Bazil – I'll start with you – when did you realize the zombies in your backyard were your parents?"

"I recognized them immediately..."

"How did that go?"

"It's not every day your parents came back from the dead and pay you a visit..." Bazil laughed...

"I can't even imagine..."

"I wasn't happy..."

"That's understandable..."

"After I recognized who they were we started arguing..."

"Oh so you were angry..."

"I was until they explained why they were there..."

"Beautiee – what was going through your mind when you saw them for the first time?"

"If I used drugs – I'd swear I was hallucinating!" she laughed...

"I bet..." Tara laughed...

"I looked out the window and I was thinking what the hell is he doing?"

"What were you expecting?"

"I have no idea!" Beautiee laughed... "That's why I went downstairs to find out..."

"Oh so you were listening to them argue?"

"No – by the time I got downstairs, they were having a conversation..."

"Okay – wait a minute – you're listening to your husband have a conversation – with zombies – and you weren't freaked out?"

"Before I married Bazil I was a different person... but now..." she said as she took Bazil's hand and squeezed it..."

"Awww..." Tara sighed...

"I don't know where I'd be if it weren't for my wife – it's a miracle she didn't run off screaming..." Bazil said...

"I would've!" Tara exclaimed...

"Once I knew it was his parents, I wasn't afraid or angry..." Beautiee said...

"What did they look like?" Tara asked...

"They looked like my parents – a little dirty but still my parents..."

"I'm imagining something like what you'd see in the Walking Dead..."

"No – they weren't decomposed..."

"That's amazing..."

"That's one of the reasons I was able to hug his mother right away..." Beautiee said...

"I'm sorry – did you just say you hugged his mother?"

"I hugged them both..."

"Wow..."

"Bazil didn't want me to at first..."

"Why's that Bazil?"

"I can't explain it – they were dead – I didn't know what would happen – but when I saw my wife hug my mother – I ran to hug my father – and..." Bazil couldn't finish. Beautiee pulled him into a hug and held him for a few moments...

"I can't imagine what that must've been like..." Tara said...

"They were a little boney, but not like skeletons..." Beautiee said...

"I missed my parents so much – I was so happy to be able to hug them again..."

"I still can't believe it..." Tara said...

"I feel like God gave me another chance to do something for them and I'm happy we were able to help them..." Bazil said...

"Is that how you feel Beautiee?" Tara asked...

"I'm so happy we could do that for his parents. I'm glad I got to meet them. This whole experience has brought us closer..." Beautiee said as Bazil took her hand and they looked at each other...

"Oh wow – that's beautiful. Thank you so much..."

"You're welcome..." Bazil said...

"I'm Tara Rosenbloom, News 12 Westchester. Thanks for watching..."

"We're clear..." the cameraman said...

"Thank you so much for doing this interview..." Tara said as she got up...

"You're welcome – is it okay if I give you a hug?" Beautiee asked...

"Absolutely..." Tara said as they hugged each other..."

"Thank you Tara..." Bazil said as he pulled her into a hug...

"Umm – okay..." Tara laughed as she hugged him back... "I wasn't expecting that..."

"We're ready Tara..." the cameraman said...

"Okay – thanks again..." Tara said as they left...

"Come here Mrs. Osgood..." Bazil breathed as he pulled her into a kiss..."

"Bazil & Lydia had a love that stood the test of time. This is the beginning of their eternity. Thank God we were able to give them their happy ending. I hope you enjoyed this story... I sure did..." Beautiee read out loud as she saved the final edits, sent the book off to be printed, logged off, closed the laptop, got up from behind her desk, and went over to Bazil...

"I love you so much..." Bazil said as he pulled her close to him and rubbed her stomach...

"I love you too..."

"You ready to go to bed?" he asked, smiling mischievously...

"Yes... I'm ready..." she sighed as he kissed her and then he took her hand and led her out of the library.